New World Order

NEW
WORLD
ORDER

stories by Derek Green

9/12/10

PITTSBURGH

Autumn House Press

PITTSBURGH

Autumn House Press Staff
Executive Editor and Founder: Michael Simms
Executive Director: Richard St. John
Community Outreach Director: Michael Wurster
Co-Director: Eva-Maria Simms
Fiction Editor: Sharon Dilworth
Special Projects Coordinator: Joshua Storey
Associate Editors: Anna Catone, Laurie Mansell Reich
Assistant Editor: Courtney Lang
Editorial Consultant: Ziggy Edwards
Media Consultant: Jan Beatty
Tech Crew Chief: Michael Milberger
Administrator: Rebecca Clever
Volunteer: Jamie Phillips

ISBN: 978-1-932870-22-0
Library of Congress Control Number: 2007943445

All Autumn House books are printed on acid-free paper and meet the international standards of permanent books intended for purchase by libraries.

This project was supported by the Pennsylvania Council on the Arts, a state agency, through its regional arts funding partnership, Pennsylvania Partners in the Arts (PPA). State government funding comes through an annual appropriation by Pennsylvania's General Assembly. PPA is administered in Allegheny County by Greater Pittsburgh Arts Council.

For my family

and in memory of Juan Colón

After all, life teems with things that have no earthly reason.

Saki, "Reginald's Drama"

Acknowledgments

I owe my deepest gratitude to Andrea Beauchamp, ideal reader and even better friend. Thanks also to Sharon Dilworth, Michael Simms and everyone else at Autumn House Press. And to Jill Bennett Anderson and Noelle Calvillo. Finally—to Maggie, Jack, Mac, Emma.

Contents

New World Order

The Terms
of the Deal

I had been in Baghdad, in the Green Zone, for a year and a half when word came down that one of my clients was dead, killed in action. This was always bad news, for obvious and not so obvious reasons. No one wanted to see a young man die. But it also meant a deal was blown, a contract had to be reverted, cash would come out of my pocket.

Clarence Brinkman, I read from his file, Private First Class, all of twenty-three years old. According to my handwriting, PFC Brinkman had placed an order for a Harley Fat Boy with all the trimmings: custom skirted back fender, low-riding Badlander seat, polished chrome shotgun exhaust. A sweet machine, and expensive, on an E-2 pay grade. Private Brinkman must have really wanted that bike. I tried to remember who he was—I could, sometimes, even months after a deal. But Brinkman from Dayton brought nothing to mind. Just another sad story and one more lost commission. I stamped the file DECEASED. Military mail would carry it out to Dubai and from there to home office in New York, and that would be the end of that.

Or so I thought.

A week later I was sitting with a dog-eared *Playboy* on my desk when the door to my trailer opened. A soldier strolled in, a big guy in standard ACU fatigues and dusty desert boots. He nodded my way, then clomped around the room, wrists crossed at the small of his back. Not much to see: some posters on the wall, a few glossy product brochures—new cars, trucks, motorcycles. A humble showroom, though not so bad for a combat zone.

The man didn't speak at first: enlisted men could be shy and painfully polite around civilians. He wore a pair of hard stripes on his shoulder, two up, a rank you didn't see all that much—a true corporal. Stars and bars was the first thing we learned: shoulder insignia meant rank and rank meant pay grade and pay grade gave you a very good idea of what a prospect could afford to buy.

He finished browsing and took a position beside my desk, looking down at the open magazine. "That redhead one of the products you got for sale here?"

"Don't we wish," I said. The second thing you learned: move your conversation toward a deal. "To be honest, you look more like a Harley man to me. I'd suggest a Soft Tail Special, if you like her."

He took the seat across from me. Small blue eyes stared out from his sunburned face. A big guy, as I said, but with the pimply stubble of a kid. When he clasped his hands on the desk in front of me I saw the thick, scarred knuckles of a combat soldier. Massey, read the name tape above his right breast.

"I've seen guys buy jewelry in the Green Zone for their girlfriends back home, or a Persian rug, or even get a damn foot massage. Hell, I eat at Burger King about every other day. But I'm gonna tell you the truth. I had no idea you all sold cars here too."

"And motorcycles," I said. "Harley-Davidson, Buell. American legends."

"American legends," he said with a smile. "On sale right here."

"Only the best in the world." I took out a prospecting sheet and penciled his name in the top box. "Mind if I ask how you came to find out about us, Corporal Massey?"

"In fact, I don't," he said. "Buddy of mine bought a motorcycle from you guys a while back, on installment plan—Military Advantage Program, I think you call it. He was scheduled to take delivery at his parents' place one-hundred and twenty-two days from now. Ended up KIA, though. Named Brinkman."

I placed the pencil in front of me and laced my own fingers. "I remember him," I fibbed. "Clarence, PFC. I was real sorry to hear about that, Massey."

"Yeah, me too," he said. "But, hey. Shit happens."

What could I add to that? Shit did indeed happen.

"So my question is, Brinkman being dead, what happens to that motorcycle?"

"To the motorcycle? I'm not sure I'm following you, Massey."

The man leaned forward, elbows to knees. His beady eyes focused on me and I imagined him on patrol, rifle high, gaze locked—not someone to mess with lightly. "It's a pretty simple question, sir. What happens to the bike? It was ordered. It must have been built. His payments were up-to-date—all that money paid right on time. So where's the bike?"

"Well, I'm not sure, Massey. I mean, the contract was what we call reverted—that means basically the order was cancelled, and the money would have been returned."

"To a dead guy."

"Well, no. To the next of kin, I guess. I suppose it would depend on what he had arranged in the case of his, you know—"

"Yeah, I know."

"But the bike itself? I would imagine that goes back to the manufacturer." To be honest, I wasn't sure what happened to the actual machine. I wasn't all that interested either.

"What if I told you I wanted to buy that bike?"

"You mean a bike *like* that one?"

"Come on, man. I mean *that bike*." He had an odd, unpleasant grin. "I want to I buy it myself."

"Those payments have been cancelled, Massey." I had picked my pencil back up and was tapping it on the desk in suspicion. "This man's family or the Army or someone has that money."

"You're not hearing me," Massey said. "I don't want the money. I want the bike."

"But the bike is gone. For all I know, it's been sold to someone else or disassembled and put back on the shelves in some factory back home."

"Well, there must be some kind of ID number for it, right? You could at least look that up."

"Okay," I said. "Fair enough. There's a VIN for it, assuming it was ever built."

"You do me a favor. Look into it for me. If you find that bike, I'll buy it." He climbed to his feet. "In fact, what would you say if I told you this: you get that bike for me, I can get eight, nine other guys come in and buy ones just like it from you."

Yeah, right. I leaned back and clasped my hands behind my head, wondering what I had here, whether joker or thief. "Why, I'd say that would be just great, Massey. I'm always looking for new business."

"I figured you might say that." He passed a card with contact information over my desk. "You fill in your little sheet there, and get back with me, let me know what you find out. Deal?"

"Sure. Deal."

He gave a curt military nod, plunked a patrol cap on his shaved head, and wandered back out into the heat and the dust.

Exchange Motor Sales had a simple mission: sell vehicles to soldiers. A captain stationed overseas gets a call from his wife that the minivan just died back home? We could cut him a deal for a new one right there on base in Okinawa or Mainz, wherever, and arrange for spot delivery stateside. Some poor grunt wanted a dream machine—a Harley all decked out, say, as reward for simply staying alive? We offered easy installment plans.

The outfit was technically part of the military post-exchange system, the PX, base stores where soldiers bought everything from uniforms and underwear, to washers and driers. We were owned by Mason Group Worldwide and operated under an act of Congress. Wherever there were active military personnel, we could be found—at permanent bases in the States and overseas, at embassies and border outposts, on the DMZ. We even had agents stationed on battleships and aircraft carriers—and in the middle of combat zones.

The company kept a low profile and I had heard of the job from a friend of a friend. I was a strong candidate: some school, some sales experience; no close family, not even a dog. I had a good interview and they laid out the terms of the deal: for a two-year commitment to work in Iraq, wherever they needed to send me, I would be paid $10,000 a month plus commission—tax-free, room and board provided. They wanted to be clear: this was a highly undesirable assignment, extremely dangerous. But with incentives, bonuses and some luck, I could walk away with nearly half a million. And for what it was worth, added my interviewer, not a single one of their agents had been killed in any theater in nearly a decade.

I sat on a commercial airliner to Dubai, a charter to Kuwait City, then a rough flight on a C-130 waiting to get shot from the sky. We made the harrowing dash from Baghdad International Airport to the Green Zone in armored vehicles with armed military escort—the most dangerous five miles on earth, they later told us.

Our regional director was Dick Sprowl, Chief Warrant Officer, USMC, retired—lean and mean, straight as an arrow, a boss you paid attention to. He briefed eight of us in a paneled room once used to hold state dinners for murderous dictators. We were in an active combat zone, he said, as if we needed a reminder. While we would be working in the relative safety of forward bases, we were nonetheless at all times in extreme danger. Each of us stood to make a small fortune, and there were only a few rules. Number one, stay alive. "Because money don't mean shit if you're dead." That led to number two: "Under no circumstances, not for any reason whatsoever, do you go off base. Not for sightseeing, not for whores, not to help a baby stranded on the goddamn side of the road. I find out you left base and somehow made it back alive, I'll kill you myself." And number three: "We're running a business here. Keep scrupulous records. File orders on time. Shoot straight. Don't fuck with the money." Sprowl gave a hard glare. "Break a rule and you're gone," he said. "Finished. Kaput. Contract null and void. And I'll make it my personal mission to make sure you don't get a penny of that precious money you're risking your lives for."

Sprowl hopped back to Dubai and the other agents fanned across the country to their bases. I spent my first night alone in a dusty trailer with a broken air conditioner, contemplating the mistake I had made. But you can get used to almost anything. I met a few people, made a few deals. I bought an air conditioner at the PX and spent my days trying to make contacts, get word out that we were operating on base, right there in Baghdad.

The Green Zone was an American bubble, four square miles surrounded by razor wire and blast-proof walls in the middle of a ruined city. The area had been the seat of government, a place where the wealthy and well-connected had lived in villas on manmade lakes, where military parades were held every other weekend, and man-eating lions were kept as pets. After the statue of Saddam fell, there was a scramble to occupy the buildings that hadn't been destroyed. Central Command was set up in the Royal Palace, villas were converted to barracks. The gracious mansions of dead Baathist party members had become offices for the huge American contractors—Halliburton, KBR, Mason—and fancy homes for their executives. A coalition of the billing, ran the joke. And it was true: there was more money to be made on the frontlines than anyone could imagine.

I occupied the long evenings drinking beer, studying product information, and learning the intricacies of my contract: the small base allowance we received in cash; how we accrued dollars toward our monthly salary, which was to be paid out in full upon completion of the two-year commitment; how we earned bonus points on top of that. When bombs exploded in the distance, or when news came of a client's death, I reminded myself of my own small dream: a piece of land in a place where the leaves turned in the fall and snow fell in winter—an old farmhouse, a tidy bank account, maybe even a dog. I gradually built myself into one of the top producers outside of the States, and counted down the days till I was done.

Each month Sprowl notified us by e-mail of a new incentive program, some product to push, for extra commission. It so happened that the month Massey walked into my office we were having a Harley contest. Motorcycles were high-commission units to begin with. Even if the young corporal could deliver only a couple of the referrals he promised, it would be like closing half-a-dozen deals. So I copied down the VIN from Brinkman's file and got on the phone to Dubai.

"What do you mean he wants the same bike?" Sprowl growled into the telephone. "Bullshit. Tell him we'll sell him one just like it. What's the difference?"

"I thought of that myself, Dick. But he was pretty insistent. He wants the very same bike. I think the guy who got killed was a buddy of his so, you know, maybe it's a sentimental thing."

"Buddies, huh?" One thing about Sprowl: he was into honor and army buddies and all of that. He was on the up-and-up too, a buttoned-down man, completely honest. I didn't even think to suggest tricking Massey by selling him a different bike without saying so. "Well, shit. All right, slick. I'll see what I can do."

Two hours later Sprowl was back on the phone. He'd found the bike. "Hasn't even been processed yet, if you can believe that," he said. "God-damn New York office."

"Go ahead and fax over the paperwork."

"Negative," Sprowl said. "You'll need original copies to move title from your decedent to the new client. Go ahead and get the transfer going, and I'll carry paperwork on my person when I come through next week. Oh, by the way," he added, "since the deal was already started, I hope you know I can't count it toward this month's contest."

"Hey, Dick," I said, "far be it from you to ever bend a rule, right?"

I called Massey the next morning with the news. He seemed neither pleased nor displeased, as if he'd expected nothing less than me finding this needle in a haystack for him. He asked if he could come in that afternoon to get his paperwork started.

"I'll be sitting at this desk for the next four months," I said.

"Check," he said. "I'll be there at four P.M. sharp."

He walked in right on time—followed by four other GI's, each one larger than the last. These bearish young men clustered around my desk like oversized furniture. They flipped through glossy manufacturer brochures and perused our detailed pricing sheets. I duly recorded their names—Veeris, Utley, Becker and Dobbs—and explained our financing plans. They nodded, exchanging observations among themselves. They jotted notes on price worksheets with the stubby little pencils I provided.

Massey took me aside after he finished his paperwork. "I would've had four more guys for you but they're heading out on night patrol. They'll be back tomorrow if you're interested in taking a few more orders. And I know you're interested in that."

"All these guys want bikes," I said, "like yours?"

"Not exactly like mine. You know—just big old Harley hogs. American legends, right?"

"What I mean is, each one of these guys wants to *buy* a bike?" I glanced over at the group, none ranked higher than private, E-3 pay grades at best. "These are expensive machines, Massey. I mean, these are the most expensive vehicles in the world on two wheels."

"I'm glad you brought that up," Massey said and draped a heavy arm around my shoulders. "Because some of these soldiers are experiencing less than rosy financial scenarios. Ain't that a bitch? I mean, these guys are out here humpin' every day, freaking combat specialists, for Christ's sake. And still they gotta worry about making ends meet." He raised his head from our huddle. "Hey, Veeris!"

Private Veeris turned away from a four-color product brochure.

"How many kids you got?"

"Three, Corporal."

"And a pregnant wife, right?"

"Correct, Corporal."

"Jesus Christ," Massey said, "best thing ever happened to you, getting shipped over here. Give that dick of yours a rest." The assembled GI's laughed. They returned to their worksheets.

"Now a guy like Veeris," Massey told me, "I'm thinking it might be a little stretch for him to buy one of these bikes, right?"

"Yeah." I was nodding. " I think it might."

"So my thought is, maybe you could work out sort of a bulk deal for us. I figure I'm bringing you a lot of business here. So maybe you can come back at me with some special prices."

"Listen, Massey. I appreciate what you're trying to do. I mean, I really do. But I can't give price breaks—no matter how many bikes you buy. We already offer rock-bottom prices."

"There's always a way to lower a price."

I sighed. "Even if I could lower what we charge—and I can't Massey, really—but let's say I could. Even if I could drop fifteen-percent, we're still looking at almost half-a-year's income for some of these guys."

"Hey, we're all good for it. These are stand-up individuals. If they sign a contract, they're gonna live up to it."

I lowered my voice. "That's not what I mean. What I mean is, I can't be selling any of these guys things they can't afford."

"Yeah, well, we all talked that over," Massey said. "We're aware of how expensive these motorcycles are. Like I said, it might be a stretch for some of us—" here he showed his grin again "—which is why I'm asking for a special deal. But no one's doing anything that's gonna get them in trouble."

I glanced over my shoulder at his group of privates. They had begun to relax, trading insults, joking around. I must have looked unconvinced: when I turned back, Massey drew me into a one-armed bear hug.

"Here's the thing," he said. "This soldier, Brinkman, the one whose bike I wanted you to track down? He had this idea a few months back. He found out about your operation here and he decided we should all buy one of these motorcycles. Pay now, drive later—you know, when we were out of this goddamn hellhole and finally back home. He figured we'd all meet up, maybe a year after we were out, take these hogs on a trip across the country, our own little version of Hell's Angels."

The man smelled of dust and sweat.

"We thought it was a pretty stupid idea, to be honest—like you said, these are damn expensive bikes, even with the 'rock bottom' price you guys supposedly offer. But Brinkman went ahead and did it himself. He said he figured we'd come around. Once he got killed, it didn't seem so stupid after all. In fact, it seemed like a pretty damn good idea—like a dream, you know? Meet up one day—nine, ten of us—and head out on the open road. Just drive across the whole damn country, rockets under our asses and wind in our faces." He had a slightly demented laugh. "I mean, we'd form a band but none of us knows how to play a fucking instrument. Right?"

He released me. What was I going to say to that? I sighed once more. "Listen Massey, I want to sell you guys these bikes. Believe me, no one wants you to buy them more than me."

"And that makes me feel real good."

"But I'm not in control of much—I'm not in control of anything, actually. I can get creative with financing. And I can help push through an iffy deal. But I can't make promises about getting a lower price."

"Hey, you'll do what you can," he said, and clapped my back. "Anyway, all we're talking about right now is filling out a few applications. That doesn't cost anything, right?"

"Just my time," I said.

"What, you got something better to do?"

So I took four new applications for four new bikes—a week's worth of business in the space of an hour. And according to Massey, more was on the way. I stapled the last order and slipped it into a stiff manila envelope and told the soldiers that I would get back to them as soon as the applications could be processed.

That was when the private called Dobbs whistled through his teeth and spoke up. "Five Harleys, at the price you're charging? You must be making a pretty fat commission on that."

"I do depend on commission," was my practiced answer.

"Boy, oh, boy," said PFC Utley with a broad corn-fed grin. "How much you making out here? I bet you're pulling down fifty, sixty grand a year." Utley said this the way he might comment on some overpaid athlete's income—not in rebuke, just good-natured amazement that some people were destined to make so much more money in this life than he was—the way some men accepted that it would always rain on their day off.

Private Dobbs wore a skeptical grin that was less accommodating. "Motherfucker," he said. "And we're out there on combat patrols keeping his ass safe. For less than half of that." His grin hardened into something nastier. "I guess the joke's on us."

"Hey," Massey said, "this is an educated man, Dobbs, not some fuck-tard from Compton." Everyone, including Dobbs, laughed. "You signed up for your deal, and he signed up for his. So drop it."

Which brought the discussion to a close.

Massey came through with the other four members of his squad later that week, as promised, and an extra pair of grunts from another squad over the weekend. He must have been one convincing corporal.

When Sprowl arrived from Dubai on Tuesday, the paperwork was waiting for him in a neat stack on my desk.

"Twelve deals in three days?" Sprowl said, looking through the folders. "Bullshit. What are you doing out here, blowing GI's in the urinals?" He allowed himself a bark of laughter for the witticism.

"Superior salesmanship," I said. "Listen, there's a request I need to make."

"The answer is no."

"Some of my buyers, as I'm sure you'll see, are a little dicey in the cash department. So what I'm wondering is whether we can work some kind of volume deal for them, as a group, something from the manufacturer."

"What are you out of your fucking mind? We're not running a charity here."

"It's just that they're hoping to purchase as a unit. So I thought maybe something could be worked out. That's a lot of deals, boss."

"Hey," he said, "you're feeling so generous, donate your commission to the cause. But the prices stay the same."

Sprowl's visits were big social events for me. I put out a sack of burgers and a case of beer, and we worked through three months' worth of paperwork, the occasional explosion sounding in the distance. Sometime after midnight Sprowl yawned and said it was time to knock off for the night. He was scheduled to leave for our other local offices the following afternoon—Falujah, Kirkut, Basra. These sorties were made, space available, on Blackhawk convoys, which flew in three-wing formations for security reasons: if one got shot down, the second would land to attempt ground rescue, while the third provided fire cover from above.

I wouldn't have minded staying up a while longer for the company. But we both shuffled off to our cots, agreeing to get back to work in the morning.

I was awakened by air raid sirens and surreal swimming lights. I heard a hissing sound, stuttered loudspeaker static, followed by an explosion that rattled the walls of my trailer. "What's going on!" I cried.

Sprowl was in my face. "Mortar fire," he shouted. "We gotta take cover!"

I started to go for my pants which were on the other side of the room.

"Negative!" he shouted. "No time. Get the fuck *out* of here!"

I slammed through the trailer door and raced across the open plaza in nothing but my underwear. Searchlights swung wildly and sirens wailed. Soldiers in flak jackets rushed by in the opposite direction, toward the front gates, bristling with weapons. It was hot in the Green Zone but my legs had become stumps of leaden ice. Nothing like this had happened since my arrival. Despite drill after drill, I had no recollection of where the bomb shelters were located. I followed Sprowl at a run. A row of palms just ahead lit up like stage props in a flash of mortar explosion. The hair blew back on my head and my ears sang.

We came to a bunker where soldiers swung flashlights to direct us down a short flight of steps. Concrete walls reinforced with sandbags muffled the outside noise. I was covered in sweat, shivering, unable to stop my teeth from chattering. Twenty or thirty other civilians shared the shelter with us.

Sprowl sat across from me with a grim expression on his taut face; then he broke into a grin.

"You realize you're the only one in here in your skivvies?"

I saw that it was so.

"You look fucking ridiculous!" he shouted. "Man, you should see yourself!"

My teeth went chattering on.

"By the way," he said, "I forgot to mention earlier. If you close on all the deals you got this week, you'll win the Harley contest! Isn't that just great?" His grin became laughter. "Because I know how bad you want to win that goddamn contest!"

He slapped my knee and laughed on as bombs came down in the night. I freely admit that I didn't see a damn thing funny about any of it then, and I still don't now.

It was decided that the local insurgents would have hell to pay following the mortar attack. Fireteams were sent into the violent neighborhoods beyond the gates, fresh soldiers were transferred in from other bases, diplomats arrived for more talks—all of it good for business. Sprowl expedited my deals, to secure what business we could before Massey and his men were shipped out and their attention turned to graver matters.

Within a week a package arrived from Dubai. All but three of the contracts had gone through—not bad for so many applications, but not so good for the group. I sat at my desk with the files and a calculator, but no matter how I massaged the numbers, I couldn't make those three deals work. Even downgraded to our cheapest bikes, they were going to need a whole lot more money down. I was willing to take a hit on commission for two or three contracts, but even that wouldn't make up the difference. And knowing Sprowl's sense of fairness, he would insist that I offer the same deal to the entire group. My sympathy for a few jarheads didn't extend so far.

I met Massey at the base Burger King to go over the mixed results. He sipped Coke as I spoke. He nodded, then stirred the ice in the bottom of his cup.

"Three of them, huh? Damn."

I turned my hands over to show my palms. "Nothing much I can do," I said. "I'm sorry, Massey." And I was, too.

"So which three are out?" he asked.

"That I can't tell you," I said. "It's confidential."

He grinned. "Confidential," he said. "Okay, Mr. Confidentiality. So how about if I can guess the names, then you don't tell me if I'm right?"

I shrugged.

"Veeris is one, of course. Probably Utley. And my guess is Dobbs, too."

I made no response.

"But all the rest went through?" he said.

"All but three," I said. "Mind you, I'm not confirming or denying which three." But he knew he had named the right men.

"Well," he said and brought his hands down on the plastic table, a decisive gesture. "Looks like they're out, then. Too bad for them." He stood and placed his cap on his head. "Ah, what the hell. It was a long shot, anyway. Worth a try, though, right?"

He headed for the door.

"Hey, Massey," I said. "There's maybe one more thing I can try, see if I can get this through."

"Yeah?" he said. "What's that?"

"I'd rather not say. But I'll let you know if it works out. If it does, just do me a favor and ask your guys to keep their mouths shut, okay? No matter what they think."

He appraised me with his small eyes. Then he nodded. "Okay," he said. "I'll do that. You let me know how it all works out." And he walked out into the crowded plaza.

Soldiers drilled in Victory Square just outside of my trailer. I went inside and flipped the window sign from OPEN to CLOSED. I closed the blinds against the glaring sun—an unnecessary gesture, but in keeping with what I had in mind.

I placed three manila folders on the desk and logged on to my computer. The method by which we were compensated was Byzantine, complex by design, a system of deferred payment, accrued bonuses and minimal cash disbursements intended to keep us tethered to Exchange Motor Sales for the duration of our two-year commitment. A lot of agents groused that it was unfair. But it was the deal we had signed up for. In just under twenty months I had earned almost $300,000 to be paid out at the end of my two years, tax free, held in escrow by the company. In cash I had accumulated nearly $15,000, thanks to my miserly ways, all of which I had moved electronically from Exchange to a private account. It was my money, something neither the company nor the U.S. government could touch—all I would get if I got caught breaking a company rule.

I sat for a long time, staring at the screen, then started typing directions into the computer. No one, not even Sprowl, knew the ins and outs of the Exchange contract like I did; it was as simple as typing an e-mail for me to set up funds for each of the contracts on my desk and create dummy sources for the money I was moving. As for the clients: they would see slightly different contracts simply reflecting a nice discount on the final price of each bike. First, I set up the contract of the hapless PFC Veeris, then dough-faced Utley and finally the cynical Dobbs.

The whole thing took less than an hour and cost just over eleven grand. There was, of course, the question of who I was doing a favor for. I would make much of my money back in commission and bonuses once all the deals had closed—in fact, to ungenerous eyes, it might look like some sort of kickback had been arranged, though not a very smart one on my part. The soldiers themselves would perhaps be saddled with debt that they could only marginally afford. I knew people complained about operations like ours: that we were exploiting soldiers, taking advantage of the underpaid men and women actually fighting the war, by selling them luxury items they didn't need. I saw the point, but disagreed. Who was to say how they should spend their money? Sure, this was a self-serving argument. But if they wanted to "finance a dream," as we put it in our sales literature, then why not? If it was something to look forward to—some *thing* to live for beyond this place? When you thought of it that way, what was little bit of money—or even a whole lot of it?

The GIs shuffled through the trailer one at a time. I explained the terms of their contracts, the amount to be paid monthly, how to arrange for delivery of a shiny new badass Harley-Davidson, an American legend, upon completion of their tour of duty and return to the United States. If anyone had suspicions about the contracts, they kept their mouths shut as they signed on all those dotted lines—Massey had come through once again.

The contracts were processed in Dubai, approved in New York, and that was that. Or so I thought. I got a call from Sprowl.

"I see where you got all them bike deals through," he said.

"That's right, boss. All twelve of them."

"Even those three iffy ones."

"Even those."

I could hear Sprowl chewing gum over the line. "Them three grunts somehow came up with all that money, huh?"

"Lucky sons of bitches," I said.

"Yeah, real lucky, I'd say. Almost like too lucky."

"Some guys are lucky," I said. "Some guys aren't."

I imagined his steely expression as he played out his end of the conversation. A painful silence took place. Then Sprowl said, "You give any more thought to my offer about staying on for another year? Double your money in half the time, slick."

Another year? I had a Sprowlian answer ready for that question. Instead, I opted for diplomacy. "Sorry, boss, but like I said earlier. I'm just not interested."

"I might could try twisting your arm a little bit," he said. "Couldn't I? Maybe a lot, even. Maybe a whole lot."

I had no reply. I sat there listening to the dead air over our telephone connection. Sweat had broken out on my forehead. Finally, Sprowl said, "Hornick, you wouldn't be trying to fuck me just a little bit, would you?"

"Dick," I said, "believe me. You are the last person on this planet I would ever try to fuck."

There was more gum chewing. "Well, I do believe you're telling the truth about that, ace." Sprowl paused once again. "So I guess I'll just say congratulations. You won yourself a nice little contest. Must feel real good."

"It does," I croaked.

"Real good."

"You have no idea."

The new Exchange man arrived for me to train sixty days before I was scheduled to ship back home. Things had gotten worse over the last few months and I was convinced something would happen to me before my contract was up. I stayed in a lot more; I went online a lot to count my money and calm my nerves. The day my replacement arrived—Newman was his appropriate name—a pair of guards were killed by a car bomb right at the gates of the Green Zone. I could imagine Newman at his desk, contemplating the mistake he'd made. I showed him how the ordering system worked and passed on my box of *Playboys*.

I had three weeks left when Newman came into the back room of the trailer and told me someone wanted to see me. Massey was waiting in the showroom. He stood, cap in hand, the same as the day he'd first walked in.

"Thought you might be interested to know everyone's real happy with their deal," he said. "Making payments right on time and everything. Even Veeris's wife is okay with it, long as he comes back in one piece."

"Great," I said. What was I supposed to say?

I asked what else was new and Massey explained that his unit would be shipping out in one week's time, heading north to Diyala, where security had deteriorated and fighting had grown heavy. He also told me that his entire brigade's tour had been extended, from fifteen to twenty months.

"Holy shit," I said, unable to hide my horror at the thought. "That's awful, Massey. I'm sorry I asked."

He grinned his odd grin. "Yeah, well, that's what we signed up for, I guess—the fine print, anyway." He shook his head. "Listen," he said, "I'm pretty sure I figured out what you did earlier. To get those deals through, you know?"

"No, I don't know, Massey. I have no idea what you're talking about."

He regarded me for a long moment. "Check," he said at last. "I got you." He placed his cap back on his head. "Hey, man, I was thinking. I bet you get a pretty good discount through your company, right? Why don't you spend a little money, get yourself one of these fine machines. You can meet up with us when we all get back, when you're back too, ride the open road. Like you said, American legends."

"Yeah, well, maybe."

"Maybe? Come on, commit, man. Picture it. Make it happen."

I pictured it, the group of us blasting down some highway back home, wind in our hair, thunder in our ears—all the dust and heat and fear and death finally behind us like so much paved and open road.

"Thing is," I said, " I don't even know how to drive a motorcycle. All I do is sell them."

"Figures," he said with a laugh. He stopped at the door. "It really was a good idea that kid had, wasn't it? Brinkman. Big old carrot-top from Ohio. Not a bad guy, either."

I nodded and tried once again to picture the man. But I had no recollection of him at all. Massey shook my hand then opened the door and walked out toward whatever waited for him and his men in the desert to the north.

Cultural Awareness

Patrick Pierce received the e-mail on a Monday, one of those messages broadcast to hundreds of people from some anonymous drone in H.R., a name attached to no face he would ever see. CULTURAL AWARENESS, read the subject box. The message said:

MGW staff scheduled for overseas rotation will be required to attend Cultural Awareness Training. As accredation for CAT is required to be entered into the expatriate compensation program, it is strongly recommended that you enroll now. Please indicate three choices from the meeting times below and have a great day!

Accredation, Patrick thought?

A few steps down he came to the desk of his team leader, Brenda Gilbert. She glanced up, then back at her computer. A silence took place. "What now, Patrick?"

"You get that e-mail on Cultural Awareness Training?"

She made a few clicks with her mouse. "You're going, Patrick. Everyone transferring overseas has to. *No* exceptions."

"Come on, Brenda, more *diversity* training? I learned to love the unwashed masses back in college."

She grinned. Since coming to international operations, Patrick had dated Brenda three times and slept with her once. This, they agreed, had been a bad idea.

"You wanna go overseas, you gotta take the class," she said. A pleasant mean streak showed through her smile. "It only lasts six weeks. You make *daisy* chains and learn to *trust* people from other countries."

Patrick groaned. "Get me off the hook, Brenda. Please? For old time's sake?"

She regarded him from beneath a single arched eyebrow. "Yeah, right," she said. "You read the e-mail. No exceptions. Not even for the great Patrick Pierce. You're going, my dear."

He sat back down in front of his computer. Oh well, what the hell, he thought. He selected one time-slot for the course, and one time slot only: Friday, two p.m. If they were forcing him to be brainwashed, they could at least give him a longer weekend for his trouble.

Patrick Pierce was special and he knew it. He was twenty-six, charming in a way that made people, men and women both, give him things he wanted. He held a Stanford MBA, spoke fluent Spanish and French learned from a series of east-coast nannies, had spent time between college and B-school backpacking across Europe and Australia. Patrick's father was a retired Mason Group Worldwide executive officer and his great-grandfather had been a hunting buddy of Walter H. Mason, the company's enigmatic founder. One day Mason Group would merge with a military contractor and an energy company to form one of the largest companies in the world, and Patrick truly believed he could be that company's president. He looked forward to the approaching years—three abroad and the bright career beyond—as a birthright: a time to be filled with honor, power, riches, fame, and the love of women.

He showed up late at the windowless conference room of a second-rate hotel the following Friday. The place reeked of corporate budgetary restraint. Round tables were draped with limp linen. Several flipcharts stood guard at the front of the room, near aIn front stood a table outfitted with a laptop computer and and gun projector, those instruments of pain and boredom.

Patrick carried a cup of coffee to a table near the back of the room. There were maybe fifty other attendees—drowsy-looking, bored, no one he knew.

A slim woman approached from the front, the instructor. He eyed the tweedy skirt and pale nylons. Her dark hair was pinched back in a pleasureless bun and she wore unfashionably round glasses. Patrick knew the type: freelance trainer by day, associate sociology professor by night, your basic repressed woman. Not unattractive—not at all. But uptight, probably vegetarian, certainly lonely. And she was being paid to teach *him*.

She introduced herself as the facilitator. Patrick spoke his name and shook her cool hand.

She had a strange name: Egan Shoare. She said, "You've chosen a mighty lonely spot back here. Afraid I bite?"

His eyebrows went up. "The memo I received said only nibbling would be allowed."

She surprised him once more again by not moving him to another table. With a small smile she turned on her heel. Musky perfume lingered, and as she strode to the front of the room, Patrick saw that she had delicate ankles and fine calves.

The seminar began ridiculously as such things do. Egan Shoare directed the attendees, grown men and women, to stand one by one and name their favorite cartoon character and why. An icebreaker, she called it. Patrick, nothing if not well-mannered, did as he was asked (Yosemite Sam; because of his big gun) but he drew a line at taking notes. Around him the drones laughed at canned jokes, nodded earnestly at obvious comments about customs and cultures. They scribbled away in bulky three-ring binders that Egan had handed out.

The door opened behind him. A balding head appeared, attached to a man Patrick knew, though barely, a sad-sack engineer, Rob Heeber. Patrick remembered being amused by the man admitting he didn't hadn't want to be transferred overseas but was being forced to for the job. Heeber naturally took the empty seat beside him.

"Each of you is scheduled for assignment to another country," Egan spoke in a loud presenter's voice as she swept by their table to drop a binder in front of Heeber. "But you're not only going overseas as representatives of Mason International. You're also going as Americans. The impact you'll make goes far beyond being the coworker or, more likely, the *director* of a foreign national in the employ of Mason Worldwide. You have the opportunity—some would say the responsibility—to make a positive, lasting impression on these people of different societies. By understanding the cultures and customs of the people you work with, by showing interest in them and by sharing yourself with them, you'll not only be a more effective Mason Group executive but you'll receive the inestimable gift of *personal* growth. Everyone's heard about the 'global economy' and the 'new world order' that are emerging. By the time you've completed this training, you'll better understand how all cultures in this new world are interdependent on one another and what this means to you—members of a dominant culture assigned to work in a foreign one. What will people think of you? How will you interact?"

Heeber asked in a whisper to see Patrick's binder. Patrick ignored him, amazed by the malarkey he was hearing.

"Sometimes it's hard for us as Americans to imagine that people in other countries even *have* ideas," Egan went on. "But guess what. They do. One thing we can be sure of is that *they* have an opinion about *us*—regardless of whether we can even find their countries on a map."

This offensive bit of crap actually got some laughs.

"Is there anyone in the room who can tell me three things that people in other countries might think about us Americans?"

By Patrick's wristwatch, he had endured half an hour of the class, with another two hours to go. A moment passed before it registered that Egan had said his name.

He raised his eyes.

"Your name *is* Patrick, right? You haven't participated much. I was wondering whether you can think of three things people in other countries think of us. In fact, just one would be fine."

She seemed amused. Patrick detected something predatory, almost feral, in her expression. Eyes were on him now but he made no move to sit up out of his slouch. He was willing to sit still and be quiet—to be paid to listen to the bullshit she was being paid to speak. But putting him on the spot was breaking the rules. It was rude. And two could play at that game.

"Well, I'm sure a lot of them would love to take our money, then kick us the hell out of their countries," he said, "or maybe these days just blow us up with a homemade bomb."

There were a few stifled laughs around the room. The drones were paying attention now, sensing possible mutiny.

Egan's small smile was back on display. She jotted the words *money* and *terrorism* on a flipchart, then turned to regard the participants.

"Thank you, Patrick, but I'm afraid you've jumped a bit ahead of us. Body armor won't be issued until the final session of the seminar."

This got even bigger laughs. Patrick himself grinned and turned his attention back to the doodles in his notebook.

Lady, he thought, you're mine.

Like many things, women came easily to Patrick Pierce. For him, seduction was a tool like any other—to be used with care, only when something was to be gained by using it. He was aided, true enough, by thick black hair and sleepy blue eyes, a flat stomach, and what he considered an aristocratic bearing. Patrick craved women with a sort of reckless zeal and in his experience, women mostly responded by craving him back. His sister, Denise, ten years his senior, had told him as a teenager that he was special beyond good looks; and Patrick of course had agreed. Her girlfriends fawned over him and one, a strange quiet girl of twenty-two, deflowered him when he was fifteen. Like living overseas, women were an important part of his fuzzy but bright life-plan. When Patrick thought of foreign cities, which he did a lot, he viewed them as expressions of their women: the steamy heat of Caracas, the homely but friendly abandon of Sydney. He believed his success with women was founded on understanding and appreciating them. Other men didn't see women this way; Patrick felt they were at a disadvantage to a man who did.

The seminar was over and the drones were filing from the room. To Patrick's surprise, Egan approached his table. His table partner, Heeber, smelled trouble and bailed.

"I have the feeling that we've gotten off to a bad start," she said. Something, maybe Heeber's retreat, had conjured up her small smile. "I suspect it's because we probably disagree on just about everything there is to disagree about. But I wanted to say—maybe we can start over."

Patrick had intended to wait around and approach her in the relative anonymity of the hotel corridor and he knew enough to seize an opportunity when it appeared. He said, "I had the same thought. I wanted to ask you if I could buy you a drink sometime."

She studied him for an uncomfortable period of time. "No, I want to buy you one," she said. "Only not here at the hotel. I know a place not far away."

"You mean right now?" Patrick immediately regretted the question.

"Are you busy or something?"

Well, no, he wasn't.

"So follow me."

He pulled into the parking lot of a place called Mad Buck in the snazzy little suburb of Bradford Oaks. Vexed, he looked around for the soulless car of Japanese origin that he had lost in traffic five minutes earlier. He finally spotted it, parked, climbed out. A warm September breeze had stirred trees to life and set them whispering angrily on their their grassy parking-lot islands.

Patrick blinked away dimness to see that Mad Buck's interior walls displayed antique photos of big game hunters and pelts of zebra and leopard. From above a vast schist-clad fireplace protruded the largest elk's head he had ever seen. Patrick was momentarily transported to the smoky den of his family's vacation home up in Michigan. In his disorientation, he didn't see Egan. Then he realized that she was the woman with long black hair in a corner booth near the bar.

"Hope you're hungry," she said as he slid onto the bench across from her, "because I'm starving." According to the menu the place served game of a strange sort: eel and otter, rattlesnake. The bartender came to their booth.

"Bring me a Scotch on the rocks," Egan said, "and an order of the buffalo appetizer, rare please? Do you want something?"

Patrick asked for beer. He shrugged after a moment and said, "How's the alligator here?"

"Just beautiful," the bartender said.

The man left with their order and Egan fired up a cigarette. "These seminars make me crave red meat." She exhaled a cloud of smoke, she smiled. "I wasn't sure whether you'd find me again when you got lost out there."

He resisted the urge to point out he hadn't been *lost*, exactly. Instead, he said, "I must admit, Egan Shoare, I'm very surprised."

"By...."

"This place, for one thing. You. I mean, *Scotch*?"

She peered at him through smoke. "Patrick Pierce."

"Do you remember the names of everyone who attends your seminars?"

"Of course. You might have noticed, had you been paying any attention at all." The bartender dropped off drinks. "Let me guess. You think I'm P.C., and you've heard all this cultural awareness stuff before. I'm an outsider, a freelance carpetbagger hired by the company to satisfy some stupid H.R. requirement. You think everything we talk about in my seminar is just a joke."

Patrick grinned, guilty-as-charged. "Also that you were a vegetarian. You know, Egan the Vegan."

"Wrong again." The small smile was back, behind a gauze of smoke. She pointed at him. "And yet I know all there is to know about you."

"Is that so?"

"You're a rich kid. Spoiled, but in a good way. You wear very nice suits, even on Fridays—even to training seminars. So you're ambitious. You're polite, to a point, and very well-polished. My guess is your father has a very important job for Mason Group or one of the big energy companies." She jabbed the ashtray with her cigarette. "He probably wants you to stay in the States but you can't *wait* to get out of the country and make your own mark. Nowhere too dangerous, of course—you're on your way up."

"So you're a mindreader. Or do you just investigate the people who come to your seminars?"

"What's to investigate?" She sipped her drink. "You're an open book. When do you leave the country?"

"Just as soon as this class is over."

"Less than two months away. You must be very excited. So where do you go, Patrick Pierce?"

This was a subject Patrick enjoyed and he felt the game moving back to his turf. "I was going to Argentina but the economy tanked. So it's Mexico for me."

"Is that considered very glamorous?"

"It's a big operation, and high-profile, for someone my age. I can live with it."

She actually ate buffalo meat when it arrived and listened as Patrick talked more about himself: the house he'd lined up in Santa Fe, his decision to spend the coming Christmas touring South America with friends, his languages, how well he was suited for the job wherever he wanted to go.

She pushed away her plate and looked Patrick over as if for the first time. Her eyes were large and feline without the funny glasses; in the dimly lit bar they looked black and deep like the mouths of cauldrons.

"Let me ask you something," she said. "Do you ever *question* any of this—are you ever just unsure?"

Patrick became careful. "Unsure about what? Myself?"

She waved her hand as if gnats hung in the air between them. "No, I mean about this, all of—*this.*"

"I'm stumped, Egan. I don't know what *this* all is."

"I mean the whole thing you're talking about. Going to other countries, working in Mexico. Do you ever wonder whether you're just exploiting people who have less than you do? That we're taking advantage of our strength and wealth to make ourselves stronger and richer?"

"Ah, finally," Patrick said, "more cultural awareness."

She started to light another cigarette then changed her mind. "No, really, I'm curious. Mason is this huge thing, this mysterious—*thing* with tentacles that reach all over the world. It touches thousands, probably millions of people."

"Cool, huh?"

"I guess. Unless you're living on slave wages in some third-world hellhole so rich people can make themselves richer on fat government contracts."

"We build bridges and provide electricity for hospitals," he said. "We train teachers and engineers and offer people in those countries jobs and opportunities. You know—'the company that teaches the world to farm and fish.'"

"Come on, Patrick, you're smart. You don't really believe your own P.R., do you?"

Patrick was shaking his head. "I don't believe Mason Worldwide or other big companies are the root of all evil or that some group secretly rules the world. That's *your* P.R. I don't believe that if someone somewhere is poor it's because I'm rich."

"And what if you're wrong? What if it *is* a zero-sum game and we *are* rich at their expense?"

"Then I would say I'm glad it's them who's poor and not us."

This time she did light her cigarette. "That's what I'm talking about," she said. "What an American attitude! We're right and *screw* the rest of the world."

"Well...," Patrick said.

"There's a word for that. It's called *arrogance*. Don't you have a problem with companies peddling gas guzzling SUVs like yours out there to drug lords in other countries?"

He showed his hands, helpless. "Drug lords need cars too."

"Today in the seminar you mentioned terrorism, how people in other countries want to hurt Americans?"

"But are happy to take our money." He smiled. "Is this how we get off on a better start?"

She studied him closely. The greenish light in the bar exposed delicate lines around her eyes and a dimple on her forehead that creased when she concentrated. "Where do you think terrorists get their ideas from, Patrick?"

"They're different," he said.

"Oh, really?"

"They're not normal people. They're motivated by fanaticism," he said. "Cruelty, jealousy."

"How about rage and desperation? How about frustration?"

She said this with a jaunty tilt of her head and Patrick felt a flash of real anger. "That's such bullshit. You can feel rage, and you can feel frustration. But that doesn't translate into killing people just to make a point."

"But it's okay to kill people as long as you do it in the name of free markets. Now *that's* bullshit."

"You know, I get very tired of this constant anti-American crap. We keep the economy humming around the world, we provide food and aid all over the place and what do we get in return?"

"Wealth, for one thing. Power. Adoration."

"They hate us out there!"

Her smile seemed sad—or maybe just condescending. "That's the thing. They don't hate us. They probably should, but most don't."

He wanted to bring up his travels, to point out all the places he'd been and establish his authority here. Only he was just a touch confused, because wherever he had traveled the people he met didn't hate him. And he'd seen Americans abroad who certainly deserved to be hated. And yet, and yet…. There was a point he wanted to make here, but he couldn't think of it.

Instead, he said, "How about you, Egan? You work for us, don't you? Or are you doing these seminars for free coffee and cookies?"

"At least I try to enlighten people like you."

"There's a word for that." He regretted the note of triumph in his voice, but only a little. "It's called *hypocrisy*."

She sighed and studied the air off to her right side. "We don't know each other well enough to argue like this."

"Then let's get to know each other better," he said. And he shut his mouth to study her reaction.

She watched him from behind the smoke. He couldn't tell what she was thinking but he intended to wait as long as it took for her to say the next words.

She was saved by the bartender who appeared like a troll with the bill.

"When the two of you are done saving the world, could you pay for this? It's time for me to go home."

Patrick reached for the tab. "Let me," he said.

"No—" Egan's hand slipped under his and clutched the bill first. Her nostrils had flared slightly and he imagined her legs crossed primly beneath the table. "It's on *me*."

Patrick Pierce believed he understood women because he knew he would never understand them. He decided he didn't like Egan Shoare very much. But he still wanted to sleep with her. When he called the number on her business card and suggested they meet again, she declined at first. But Patrick was used to getting his way and he knew how to persist. In the end she agreed to meet him on Tuesday and then they met again the following Saturday. They jousted about the company and Americans, about Patrick's ever-nearer expatriation, about who would pay each bill, their disagreements verging hard and sexily on argument,

Patrick thinking often of her legs under the table and growing to like enjoy her small, dark smile.

They agreed to meet a third time but she stood him up.

It was the Wednesday before the fourth meeting of Cultural Awareness, Patrick teasing that the halfway point of the grim course was cause enough to celebrate. He was seated at the bar in the Mad Buck, weighing the possible meaning of her having chosen that place again (was there some omen in coming full circle, was this the night to make his move?) when when he realized she was over twenty minutes late. He ordered a second drink and tried her cell phone but it was turned off. He tried her home phone, no answer, and left a carefully worded message. He considered ordering a third drink, but decided against it. Oh well, what the hell, he thought. He paid his bill and went home.

He checked his voicemail more often than usual the next day, a touch surprised when she failed to call. He was even more surprised to find himself thinking about her during a boring afternoon sales report meeting and while losing an after-work game of squash to his boss.

He wasn't exactly angry walking into her seminar the next afternoon but he was prepared to be. A seduction had a certain arc to it and there was certainly room for people to stand each other up and have arguments. But Patrick was a practical man: he had invested time here and he was expecting some kind of return.

He tolerated the session and his buffoon table mate patiently. He filed out with the drones afterwards but then waited for Egan in the corridor. When she emerged from the room, it was as if she expected him to be waiting there.

"I really meant to show up Wednesday," she said.

"And to return my calls?"

"That, too."

"It's simple courtesy, you know. *Professional* courtesy."

"Can we discuss this somewhere else?"

"I'm happy to talk about it here." He actually crossed his arms.

The men's room door opened and out came Heeber. He regarded first Patrick, and then the course instructor. A glow of understanding lighted the dull eyes. He scurried away.

Egan shook her head. Patrick followed as she headed for the door. "I didn't come because I *wanted* to come."

"That makes a lot of sense, Egan."

"Do you really think it's a good idea for us to see each other? I mean, speaking of professionalism? You saw your friend back there."

"He's not my friend." Patrick held the door for her, ignoring the October bite in the air. "We're both grownups. What's wrong with seeing each other? What are you afraid of?"

Egan bent her steps toward her car with Patrick in tow. When she got to the car door she turned.

"I'm not *afraid* of anything," she said. "If anything, I'm watching out for *you*."

This caught Patrick off guard and he couldn't stifle a laugh. "Oh, really?" he said. "Listen, Egan, I'm a big boy. Why not let me worry about myself?"

She waited. He still couldn't get over her ability to be two people, this guarded, prim Egan with the schoolmarm's hairdo and round wire glasses, and the other raven-haired woman he knew from their dates—if that's what they were.

She sighed, blowing air upward. "All right, Patrick. Is that what you want, really?"

"Yes," he said, "it is. So, should I follow you? To the Mad Buck?"

She squinted against the wind and the delicate crease in her forehead appeared. "Not there," she said. "Would you like to come to my house?"

His blood stirred. He resisted the urge this time to ask if she meant right now. "I would like that," he said. "Very much."

They met nearly every night for several nights thereafter. Egan's house was smaller than his apartment, artsy-craftsy: lots of wood, bookshelves. A cat lived there. Though he considered himself the seducer and despite her arrant views in matters of politics and common sense, Patrick had to admit that she possessed specific charms. These included intelligence, a supple and willing body, her small smile and scary dark eyes. In such matters, clichés applied: you could never judge a book by its cover. A dog's bark was worse than its bite.

They were lying together in her bedroom two weeks later. A window was open, its lacy curtains billowing inward and snapping back with the fitful breeze.

"I've decided," she said, "that I'm a bad person."

"You are."

"I sleep with people who take my seminars."

"That," he said, "sounds funnier than it should."

"Never with students, though, at the college." She laughed now. "Well, almost never."

"You also take money from dirty corporations."

"There is that."

"Filthy lucre."

She said, "And then there's your faults, Patrick."

"We talk about them all the time."

"It is an inexhaustible topic."

He smiled. "I've always thought my teeth were too white."

"Ah," she said, "to be so sure of oneself."

"Your trick," he said, "is to make me feel deficient unless I can come up with a list of my deficiencies. It's very clever."

"Like the paradox of the liar."

"Why do I feel like I'm about to be victimized?"

She touched his chest. "If I tell you I always lie, how can you be sure I'm not lying about that?"

"You're giving me a headache."

"The paradox is linguistic—it's just a trick."

He had closed his eyes. "I'm quite arrogant."

"Very true."

"My family's rich. But that's not a fault, despite what you think. Am I narrow-minded?"

"Shockingly. But I think mostly for show."

"For show?" He smiled. "Are you trying to make me self-conscious? I thought they were paying you to prepare me to live in another country."

"They're paying me to make you *think*. They're not paying me enough."

"Let's see. I'm arrogant. I'm narrow-minded."

"Don't forget shallow."

"And so what are we doing here? What in the world do you see in me?"

When she failed to respond he opened his eyes. He was joking, but he saw that her expression had grown dark and pensive.

"You're attractive," she said with a shrug of her slender shoulders, "you're rich. You leave the country in a few weeks, so there's no risk. What's not to like?"

The answer, to his surprise, hurt. To conceal this fact, he laughed and said, "You're a witch, I think. You cast spells."

"I'm a hypocrite. You said so yourself."

"I did, didn't I?"

"I am," she said, "a queen of lost causes."

An e-mail went out to announce a gathering at the home of Egan Shoare following the final session of Cultural Awareness. Patrick read this at his desk on the last Monday of October. Egan had told him that she always held such parties at the end of a long course. So why did it irritate Patrick so much to read the message?

At noon, Brenda Gilbert appeared at his desk.

"I thought I'd hand-deliver this," she said. "It came from travel this morning."

She passed an envelope over the cubicle wall. It contained an itinerary and a one-way ticket for Patrick's trip in two weeks.

"The great Patrick Pierce," she said. "Nearly free from the surly bonds of the U.S. of A. And we are so nearly free of him."

"What's the hell's that supposed to mean?"

"Whoa, it's just a joke, Patrick. Or do I detect a note of gloom in your voice?"

He snatched the itinerary from her hand without a word.

The great Patrick Pierce was out of sorts. He sat in his SUV for a long time after work before finally deciding to give his sister, Denise, a call. No matter that she was ten years older and lived in another city; she was the only person he ever talked to about anything even remotely personal.

They exchanged pleasantries, spoke of their parents, then Patrick got to the point. He told her about Egan and Cultural Awareness, about how they had begun to see each other, how they disagreed, argued about everything and slept together.

"And how long have you known this person?" Denise asked.

"You know, a few weeks. Not all that long."

"So then what's the problem? Love her and leave her. That's the Patrick I know and respect."

Patrick set his jaw. "There isn't a problem. That's what's gonna happen."

Denise asked when he left the country for good.

"In two weeks," he said. "I got my ticket today."

"Little brother," she said, "I think you know what's at issue here."

Bearish clouds lumbered across the sky. The phone burned against his ear. "We disagree about everything, Denise. The woman's almost ten years older than me!"

"Wow, an old bag," Denise said with a laugh. "It's classic. And it sounds to me like you got it bad, bub."

"Come on, Denise."

"I'll be very interested," she said, "in hearing how things turn out."

Patrick skipped the final session of Cultural Awareness and worked late. He had intended to skip Egan's party as well, but on his way home he found himself driving through the tree-lined streets of her little subdivision. It was a warm, windy evening two nights before Halloween. The curb in front of Egan's house was lined with fancy cars and the big SUVs she found so detestable.

People had gathered inside, coworkers Patrick now knew from class. But tonight, in this place, they seemed like trespassers. Egan, cornered by a pair of men from the seminar, smiled his way as he entered. Her gaze lingered and he felt an unpleasant trip in his chest.

He made his way to the kitchen where he fixed himself a strong drink. He took it to the table and sat alone.

"You weren't in class today."

Above him hovered Heeber's round face.

"Correct," Patrick said.

"I had to do all the exercises alone." Heeber sat; the sadness of the world seemed stamped into his doughy flesh. Patrick couldn't stand the man. "Pretty soon, we're all gonna be living in another country."

"Pretty soon," Patrick said.

Heeber extended a Tupperware box filled with cookies. "My wife couldn't come tonight," he said, "but she made these. Have one."

"No, it's okay, I don't—"

"*Have one.*"

They were large sugar cookies, round, frosted with blue seas and green continents, each a tiny map of the world.

Heeber took a bite from one of the cookies, a toothy half-moon eclipsing the southern hemisphere. Crumbs studded his thick lips. "I love my wife's cookies," he said.

Patrick needed to escape. He pushed by some people in front of the refrigerator and stepped through the back doorway. The deck was presided over by a clutch of grinning goblins and witches. Torches burned restlessly in the wind. In one hand Patrick held his drink; in the other he found Heeber's cookie, shaped like the world. He threw it into the hedge beside the house.

The screen door opened and he knew Egan was there before she spoke. She touched his shoulder. "What are you thinking about?"

"About leaving," he said. In two weeks. For three years. It struck him that he would miss these things—windy October nights, home.

"It's what you've wanted your whole life," she said. "Right? It'll be fine."

"It'll be *great*," he said.

But the words rang hollow even to him. A feeling came, something so unaccustomed that it took him a moment to name: *doubt*. He thought he should say something to Egan. He wasn't sure what—just something. But no words came. She left him listening to the wind and went back into the house.

Blood Money

**We decided to go to the desert, to
the Empty Quarter**, and try out a scheme we'd come up with for making
money. This was in Dubai, a westernized city where you can play golf on
real grass and have burgers and beer downtown at Thank God It's Friday.
The grass is kept living by a hidden irrigation system worth a fortune,
and it took two years of haggling to get a beer license from the Arabs for
a place called Thank God It's Friday. But there they were. In Dubai you
could almost forget you were in the Middle East. But at twilight, when
the sun lit one side of things and cast narrow shadows on the sand, it
was different. Wind swept in from the Saudi Desert and blew sand into
the American-style highways where there were always a few lazy camels
lounging around or a lonely figure waiting in flowing robes at the side
of the road.

Then we remembered. We were in the Persian Gulf, in another country, an Arab land with different rules that none of us truly understood.

We called our company Desert Adventures. You get the idea: load up
some Land Cruisers with a few executive souls, drive around in the sand,
pitch a night camp. For a few extra dollars or euros or pounds we were
willing to provide alcohol or arrange private belly dances.

My partner was Assad Musa, Kenya-born, raised in Egypt, educated in
Great Britain. He'd come to Dubai a few years before to race in the desert
rallies. Now he was responsible for leading our trips, keeping the vehicles
in shape and managing the Pakis—the local worker-ants who did the
heavy lifting. I'd come to the region from the States as a contractor to
help put out fires in Kuwait after the first Gulf War. By the time the fires
were out I'd made enough money to stay in the region. I headed south.
I'd learned about the desert and Desert Adventures was my idea.

We were planning a new excursion package, a dangerous expedition
for rich adventure clients tired of climbing Mount Everest—an orienta-
tion tour with limited supplies and animal caravans skirting the off-limits
Saudi frontier. We wanted all the trappings of local danger but nothing

too dangerous. A scouting trip was in order.

We packed a Land Cruiser with tents, logistics equipment and a desert box with enough food for a couple of days. At the last minute I invited someone else along—the wife of a friend of ours, Carolyn Thomas.

Right away, Assad had a problem with it.

"What's wrong with you, mate? You invite a girl without consulting me? To the fucking *real* desert?"

We both knew and liked Carolyn and her husband, Barry, who choppered executives back and forth to offshore rigs for the oil companies. He was on assignment for two weeks, I explained. I told Assad I didn't think it would be a problem for us to do Barry a favor and keep his wife company for a couple days.

Assad's smile came and went like smoke. "Whatever you say, pal. You're the brains of the operation, right?"

To get to the Empty Quarter you take the Madinat-Zayed Road west, a three-and-a-half hour trip to the edge of the desert. On the way we stopped to pick up Carolyn. She and Barry had a nice place in the city—a courtyard, some acacia trees, a pair of date palms to give it the oasis look popular around town.

Carolyn was one of those women that you found occasionally among the expats. She was refined and funny. She could discuss whatever book you happened to be reading—the kind of woman who knew, for instance, what had to be done to cap a blasting rig fire, and how dangerous the work could be. Carolyn was tall, fair-haired, freckled. Men stared. But she had the kind of self-possession that women, especially western women, needed to survive in the Middle East. And she knew and respected the desert.

She loaded her gear and climbed into the back seat. "Hello, boys. How are you today?"

"We're fine," Assad said. "Although we did have a small row earlier. My intrepid business partner here didn't bother to inform me that you were coming along until five minutes ago."

Carolyn laughed. "Advance planning? Martin, aren't you the logistics expert?"

At least, I pointed out, I'd gotten around to telling him before we picked her up.

Carolyn frowned. "Oh, my. Well, Assad, I hope at least you're happy to see me."

Assad pulled out into the traffic. His eyes flicked up to the rearview mirror. "Why, Carolyn," he said, "You know I'm *always* happy to see you."

We drove. First there was the city with its glass towers and lunch-hour traffic. To the east on the Creek loomed the huge Burj Al-Arab tower. It was a mountain of blue glass in the shape of a billowing spinnaker, the tallest hotel structure in the world, a testament to the city's wealth and ambition. Leaving town the land went gravelly. Refineries, like small burning cities, spewed smoke over vast stretches of salt-flat desert. We passed trucks loaded like cattle cars with Pakis—leathery, bent men who had been imported from the Indian subcontinent as laborers. They could be seen toiling in dirty overalls across the city in a form of legal servitude. These men lived in contrast to real citizens, people of Arabic descent, who sped by in Benzes with smoked windows at 150 kilometers per hour.

Carolyn said, "I saw the most horrid thing the other day, just inside the city."

We waited.

"This place," she said. "Sometimes I don't know."

Carolyn had been walking in the city near the gold souk when she came upon a commotion at an intersection. It was one of those scenes you see in the Middle East, the kind of thing growing up in London or the Midwest of the United States—or Mombassa, for that matter—doesn't prepare you for. Traffic was backed up, a crowd had gathered at the side of the road, and Carolyn heard what could only be described as wailing.

"At first I thought someone had been run down by a car or a lorry. Another worker or child—you know that area. Got a surprise though. It wasn't a person who'd been struck."

Assad, who'd lived here longer than any of us, said, "Let me guess. A camel?"

"It was awful. The poor beast was struggling there alone in the road."

"Hurt bad?" My addition.

She nodded. "Its legs had been broken. You know how tall the silly beasts are. Well, the car understruck it. Just awful. Someone said it looked like its back was broken too. Some teenagers were trying to give it water but of course the owner, a citizen, wouldn't let them near it. It was bleeding from the ears and moaning like a bloody *human* and trying to stand up again." She shuddered. "A veterinarian turned up before the police and offered to put the poor thing out of its misery. But the owner just let it lie there in the sun, gasping in pain. Had to settle the blood money first."

Blood money, legal restitution—a payment that had to be paid for injury or for death. It was harsh and ancient and real. If you hit someone in the road, killed or maimed someone in any way, then you were responsible for that person's responsibilities. You paid. If the person had a family, you supported the family for good. Couldn't come up with the money? You went to jail. Or worse. There had been plenty of problems. Men were known to throw themselves in front of cars, a quick exit to misery, a way to provide for the family. Insurance companies might cover you for exorbitant sums. But even then you were really at the mercy of the ruling families—you might be held responsible anyway. There were different prices depending on who was injured. If you killed an Arab of status, forget it. Next came western men and then property and women. Lowest was the working class, the true outsiders. But even hurting one of them could ruin you.

We listened to the air conditioner blowing. I said, "How long did the thing lie there?"

"Pretty bloody long. Took the police forever to arrive and the owner just stood there hovering over the poor beast and barking at anyone who came near it. I guess it finally just died and the driver, some Indian fellow, got carted away."

Assad shook his head. "Now there's the bastard I pity."

But this was the place where we had chosen to live. "That's the way it is here," I said. "We're in their country, not ours."

"Correct, Martin," Carolyn said. "But that doesn't make it any more pleasant."

We drove on, south past Abu Dhabi then west toward open desert. We listened to music on the radio until the stations faded to static. We ate some sandwiches from the desert box. Toward late afternoon wind picked up from the west, blowing veils of sand. By most standards we were in the desert but we hadn't yet reached the Empty Quarter—what Assad called the *real* desert. There were still tiny villages, police outposts, a scattering of goat or camel ranches.

A steady desert wind was blowing by the time we reached the great dunes just beyond the Liwa Oasis. We stopped and Assad climbed out of the Land Cruiser to let air out of the tires for our drive into the sand.

This left Carolyn and me alone in the car.

I said, "I'm glad you came."

She looked at me in the rearview mirror for a long time then she looked away. She seemed uncertain before she finally said she was glad to have come as well.

Assad climbed back in saying he hoped the wind would die down soon. We drove out of Liwa and headed into the deep sand. There are trails out here even in the shifting dunes. You orient yourself by permanent things—a ridge to the east, a flat plateau on the northern horizon. But with the wind blowing hard it became difficult. The storm showed no signs of letting up. The Land Cruiser's long shadow raced beside us as the desert became orange and strange.

"I can't fucking see too well," Assad said. "Damn it."

We had hoped to pitch camp just into the Empty Quarter but it was looking bad.

I said, "How do we feel about sleeping in the car?"

Carolyn laughed and said, "If we want to get bloody buried in sand."

I turned on the radio but all we got this far out was static.

Assad said, "Martin, isn't there a place a few kilometers ahead? A research outpost, I think. Do you know it?"

I remembered an odd little place—a last stop for oil researchers or soldiers on their way into the Empty Quarter. We decided that if the wind got much worse we'd try to reach this place.

Half an hour later it was dark and the wind was driving as in a snow storm. Weather was notoriously difficult to predict out here. Wind patterns shifted without warning and mountains of sand moved with them. We decided against setting up camp and made for the outpost. I took a GPS reading. I could only guess at the coordinates of the little outpost.

For a while it was unclear whether we'd be able to find the place. None of us was frightened exactly. But I admit we were relieved when we finally saw light—soft, diffuse, a London fog hovering in darkness ahead. It was impossible to see the camp until we were at the edge of the natural bowl in which it was located. The camp itself was a dozen or so small barrack-like huts clustered around a larger central building. A pair of lamps glowed forlornly, greenish light seeping into the darkness.

"How thoughtful," Assad said as we descended into camp. "They've left lights burning for us."

We parked. Carolyn and I followed Assad through a scouring wind to the central building, where an office light glowed. The camp's caretaker spoke for a while with Assad in Arabic. He was a small man in traditional clothing—leather sandals, a plain white *dishdasha*, and the brimless embroidered cap worn by the Omani people. He greeted Assad and me, kissed us on both cheeks. He ignored Carolyn.

I told Assad that we would need separate quarters for each of us.

Assad translated. The caretaker finally acknowledged Carolyn. He frowned but didn't say anything.

Assad's eyes gleamed unpleasantly. "Shouldn't the three of us board together? Save some money?"

"Tell him," I said. "Separate quarters."

It was still early. We dropped off our gear then met at the mess in the central building. It was a small room with a low table surrounded by hard, flat pillows in the Arabic style. There was a collection of coffee urns on the wall, some rugs hanging beside them, an ornate shisha pipe in the corner. And there were two other men, a peninsular Indian, it appeared, and an American, already seated at the table. They looked young to my eye, like a pair of backpackers, the type you see bumming around Bangkok or Sydney. But they turned out to be researchers—geologists, they said. We chatted. We told them about our scouting trip. They both looked at Carolyn, then away.

The caretaker was called Hazem. He brought a dinner of roast lamb, lentils and brothy soup.

The American, Pete-something, from Cal Tech, said he sure could use a cold beer. Desmond, his partner, had grown up in Goa, he told us, on the coast, and studied in Mumbai. This was his first trip to the Empty Quarter and the pair was planning to meet up with a research team some time later that week.

Carolyn said, "And what do you think of the desert so far, Desmond?"

The Indian smiled. "I could use a cold beer."

We all laughed. The wind howled outside. Sand pelted the windows. We ate and afterward we talked.

Pete the American said, "You know, our cell phones don't work at all out here."

Assad said, "You're out of range of everything, mate. There's really not much to be covered way out here."

Desmond nodded. "We have computers, fax machines—and nowhere to connect them."

Carolyn tipped her head in Hazem's direction. "Perhaps you could ask the concierge for a high-speed connection."

We laughed again. On the pillow beside Desmond was a fancy-looking camera. I nudged Assad, nodded at it.

"That yours?" Assad said.

Desmond nodded.

"I'd get it out of sight before the caretaker comes back around."

Desmond's dark eyebrows went up.

"The Arabs, they can be funny about cameras, especially near the borders."

He shrugged as if unimpressed, but put the camera back in his backpack.

Hazem brought cups of bitter green coffee. We talked some more. After more coffee we decided to turn in—there was nothing much else to do.

We said good night to our new friends. At the door of the main building we listened to the raging desert wind, a violent and desolate sound.

Assad turned to me and Carolyn before we left. He said, "Let's make it an early day tomorrow, yeah? I'd like to get the fuck out of this place and into the desert."

We agreed and went out into the night.

Our barracks were cane structures with thatched roofs, sturdy desert shacks of a type we all knew well. The temperature had been dropping the way it does in the desert. My hut was cold inside, remarkably quiet. The floor was covered with rugs and the bed was made of piled pillows and loose blankets which absorbed sound and light, a padded tomb.

Back outside wind shrieked over me and sand pelted my skin like tiny needles. I found Carolyn's hut and she let me in without a sound. The camp generator had been shut down for the evening. There was no light to be had and no heat. The darkness was absolute. My hands went to Carolyn's body. I could hear her breathing. I touched her face. The wind outside now seemed like small rain. In the dark I thought of Carolyn's face with its thin tapering nose, the dusting of freckles, her blue eyes. It was a craving I felt for her as if for food or water—a consuming desire that seemed to communicate itself to her through some subtle chemistry of nerve or sinew.

It was cold. The blankets and rugs were rough and smelled of desert. It was difficult after a while in the darkness to tell which way was up or down; the small room became a mile wide. I cupped my hand over Carolyn's mouth. I choked my own voice against her throat. We lay there together without sound in the dark and desert cold.

Sunlight blazed down. I had left Carolyn before dawn and slept briefly. Then I'd gotten back up, washed in the basin in my hut, dressed. I left my hut.

The wind had stopped hours earlier but the landscape was changed, wild and rich and strange. It was as if there had been a snowstorm the evening before. Sand had piled up against the west walls of the huts, their rounded backs hunched toward the open desert for just this reason. Our vehicles were beneath a shelter, not buried but well-scoured by sand. This was what most people envisioned when they thought of Arabia—loose, white sand that rolls like waves, the Empty Quarter, what the Arabs call the Rub Al-Khali. This wasn't the stony wasteland of the Gulf coast. This was real desert.

I walked through the dazzling light toward the central building. Inside it took my eyes a minute to adjust. Carolyn was already there, sitting with Desmond and Pete over steaming tea. She was laughing, waving her hand. She, too, had thought of snow.

"Good morning, Martin. A fine storm we've had outside, don't you think? A proper Yankee blizzard." She smiled. "Can you believe our young friend Desmond here has never seen snow?"

"This is true," he said, with his sing-song Indian accent.

"Well, you have now," I said. "Basically the same stuff. Snow's a bit lighter in color."

"And a hell of a lot colder," Pete added.

Sun burned in through the small windows. Already it was hot and I suspected the wind might become a problem again.

Desmond poured tea.

I said, "Here's the plan, Carolyn. We're packing up, digging out and heading back to the city. We'll come back when the weather's a little more forgiving."

"Leaving?" Pete sipped his tea. "Just when the fun begins?"

I laughed. I said, "We'd love to hang around with you folks. But we're out of here."

"No we're not."

This was Assad. He was coming in through the door. Behind him the caretaker, Hazem, wore a grim expression.

"What do you mean we're not leaving?" I asked. "You're the one wants to get into the desert so bad."

Assad shook his head. "It seems that we have a little problem."

We were crowded around the table. We looked at him now and waited.

"There's a pair of border guards out there, they showed up earlier this morning in jeeps. They say they've found a dead man back in the road. They want to know how he got there."

I shook my head as if to clear it, as if Assad were joking. "What?"

"You heard me," Assad said. "They've found a body."

"A body?" Pete said. "We're in the middle of nowhere."

This was not precisely true. We were on the *edge* of the middle of nowhere. But there were enough people who might have been out yesterday or the night before—herders or local villagers less than a two-day walk from this spot. There was us.

Assad seemed to read my mind. He said, "There's this place, isn't there, mate? So we're not all *that* far from civilization."

We followed Assad outside. The soldiers were standing beside a pair of boxy, air-conditioned jeeps. They were dressed in fatigues with big pistols hanging from garrison belts. They stopped chatting to look us over as we walked up. Their eyes fell on Carolyn. One of the soldiers was wearing mirrored glasses and appeared to be in charge. He spoke in Arabic to Assad.

Assad said, "He wants to know what we're all doing here. And he says they're going to want to talk to each of us separately."

The soldier kept his hands in his pockets. He jerked his head toward Carolyn and said something else to Assad.

Assad responded, "*Na'am.*" Yes.

I said, "What's he asking?"

"He wants to know whether she's married." There was a silence. "I told him of course she is."

The soldier must have assumed one of us was her husband. But he never once took his eyes off Carolyn, who stood to one side with Desmond and Pete, looking steadily back from behind her own dark glasses.

It was decided that Assad and I would go with the man in charge while his partner stayed with the rest of our group. We climbed into the back of his jeep, which he directed up and out of the bowl, plowing through drifts toward the dirt trail. I looked back toward camp. There was the cluster of buildings below us and in front of that the smaller cluster of people huddled around the second soldier's jeep.

We rode for a while in silence. Assad thought the men must be from a border patrol unit. Probably military, though they were being cagey about it. Our soldier had perceived us to be the men in charge of our odd little group and was taking us to the scene. The sand was deep in places and it was slow going. We drove for nearly an hour before we stopped. I opened the door. Heat struck like a blow.

A few meters off the roadside lay the crumpled body. The soldier gazed down, legs apart, fists on his hips. I saw how the dead man was dressed. The long white *dishdasha* and *ghutra*, both blood-stained—an abomination. This, at least, explained the fuss. The body belonged to a citizen, an Arab.

Assad took off his hat, wiped his forehead. "Christ," he said. "What a fucking mess."

The soldier spoke to Assad, who translated. The soldiers, he said, believed that the body had been here only a short time, had very possibly been dumped here after the windstorm, some time very late in the evening or earlier this morning.

I said, "*Dumped?*"

They spoke some more. The guard told Assad it looked like someone had run over the man after he was dead—the amount of blood, the way the man lay. This meant to them that someone must have left him here.

"So they think someone killed him on purpose?"

"Looks that way, mate." Then Assad said, "Of course, we're all under suspicion."

The guard was watching us from behind his shades. A smile lurked beneath his thick mustache.

"Suspicion? What the fuck of? They think one of us killed this guy? This is ridiculous."

The guard surprised me by lighting a cigarette. He spoke, letting smoke stream from his nose and mouth. Assad answered him. He spoke again. This went on for a while.

"Now what's he talking about?"

Assad shook his head.

"What?"

Assad said, "Actually, pal, he was asking if it was possible that this dead man might be the husband of our woman friend back there." Assad waited for my reaction. "I couldn't tell whether it was his idea of a joke or not. I told him no, I did not believe she was this bastard's wife."

"This is a bunch of shit," I said. "Tell this asshole to go to hell."

"Shall I tell him you're an American while I'm making demands? That should set things straight, yeah?" The guard watched closely, amused. Assad spat; he shook his head. "He wants to know where we all were last night."

I said, "We were all at camp."

"Yeah?" Assad said. "And where at camp were you, mate?"

The sun and heat were unbearable. "What the fuck is that supposed to mean? I was in my hut."

"Is that so?"

I said, "Did you come to check on me?"

Assad gazed off toward the distant horizon. The guard went on smoking his cigarette. When he finished, he threw the butt at the sand and walked to the back end of the jeep. He pulled out a plastic bag, said something to Assad and motioned with his head.

He wanted us to help get the body out of the sand. We understood: the man was testing us, watching our reactions. This was the local way. In his mind we were responsible for this dead fuck until proven otherwise. He bent over and started trying to move the corpse. I once saw a man killed on an oil derrick by a burst of gas and fire; his body had come apart like a paper doll in front of us. This reminded me of that. The body had lain in the cold through the night, then baked beneath the sun since daybreak, had become stiff and unnatural in some places, soft in others. We worked for a long time in the heat, breathing through our mouths. I sweated my shirt through. The soldier finally had to go back to his jeep for a shovel. A while later we were shoving the bag into the rear of the jeep. Then the three of us headed back toward camp.

It was afternoon by the time we arrived and the wind was starting up again, lashing at the camp, like some giant animal licking fresh wounds. Everyone had gathered back in the mess room. We sat off to one side with our little group—Desmond and Pete were there with Carolyn. Sunlight angled in through a window. The soldiers stood across the room talking in a corner with the caretaker, Hazem.

Carolyn said, "How was your little excursion, boys? Enjoyable, I'm sure."

Assad mumbled under his breath and sat with his back turned.

I said, "It appears that our friends here think one of us might have killed a man." Pete and Desmond exchanged unhappy glances.

"Lovely," Carolyn said.

The guards spoke in hushed tones to the caretaker Hazem. He nodded and looked our way occasionally in a very noncommittal way.

Carolyn said, "Well, I guess that explains why this policeman chap was so rude while you two were gone. Grilled us in Arabic the whole time and then got angry that none of us could understand."

Carolyn was tough and she wasn't going to show anyone what she was feeling. But I knew her and I knew this talk meant she was nervous. We all were nervous now. We watched as the soldiers spoke with the caretaker.

Pete said, "Listen, what can these guys do to us, I mean, really? We haven't done anything, right? We were here all last night." His partner Desmond looked on.

I said, "Actually, there's quite a lot they can do to us, Pete. None of us are citizens. None of us are Arabs. They can hold us here as long as they want. They can take our passports. They can arrest us and take us to whatever border unit they work at and hold us there indefinitely. They can exact payment, blood money, from us for that dead man out there. We're a long way from home."

Assad laughed. "Consider yourself lucky, mate. If this were Yemen or Saudi, they'd just try us and execute us on the fucking spot."

Pete licked his lips. His blue eyes darted toward Desmond, then away.

The soldiers appeared to have reached a decision. They called Assad over and started explaining something. The guard we'd gone to the desert with, the one with the mirrored glasses, did the talking. He pointed our way, he jabbed Assad in the chest, he pointed back at us. Assad listened, then came over.

He said, "The caretaker is free to go; he and one of the cops are leaving. They're taking the body away now because they're afraid another sand storm is coming. The rest of us are staying here with our friend in the dark glasses." Assad paused then. He pointed at Desmond. "Except you. They want you to go with them, too."

Desmond actually smiled a little. "Me? What for?"

Assad's jaw was set tight. "They claim to think you were spying on something out here. Our man Hazem appears to have told them about your photographic hobby."

"What are you talking about?" This was Pete. The soldiers watched silently. "He's here on legitimate research. What do they mean, *spying*? Tell them he's not going anywhere."

Assad said, "Feel free to tell them that yourself."

Desmond was scared now. Pete said we couldn't let them take Desmond.

I said, "Look, Pete, so far all they seem to want is to ask some questions. Resisting them wouldn't be a good idea."

Carolyn said, "Is it any better to let them split us up?"

I asked what the hell she thought we should do. She just looked on, impossible to read behind her dark glasses.

The first guard was ready to go. He spoke to Hazem, who disappeared behind some curtains. The guard pointed at Desmond, made a beckoning gesture.

Desmond looked at us, frightened. "What should I do?"

Assad suggested he do whatever they say.

The guard approached Desmond, took him by the elbow. Poor Desmond was wearing that friendly grin of his. "Please," he said, "can't you help me?"

Pete stood. The guard in dark glasses took a menacing step toward him. His gear—the pistol, a black truncheon—rattled on his belt. That stopped Pete. We all just stood there as the guards left with Desmond through the front door. Hazem appeared from behind the curtains with a bag. He avoided looking at us, followed the other men.

We watched through the small window as they went to the jeep with the body in it. Desmond got in and disappeared behind the dark, smoky windows.

I said, "He'll be all right."

No one responded. We watched through the window as the guard in dark glasses went over to our Land Cruiser, parked beside Pete and Desmond's own vehicle. The man shouted something to the other soldier in the jeep, jimmied open the hood of the truck, reached into the engine compartment. He walked to the Land Cruiser.

Pete said, "What the hell is he doing?"

Assad said, "They're disabling the vehicles, mate. They don't want to make it easy for us to get away."

Carolyn said, "Even I could figure that out."

Huge eddies of sand danced in the wind. The guard in dark glasses went to the jeep and stood by the window. He spoke for a while to the other guard. Then he adjusted his belt and started back toward us. The jeep lurched into the gathering clouds of sand.

Pete said, "This makes no sense. It makes no sense."

I sighed. "What makes no sense, Pete?"

"Why are they leaving us here with just one of the soldiers? Especially if they're so afraid there's another storm coming? What's the idea?" Pete paused to watch the guard in dispirited silence. "What's he going to do now?"

Soon the sky would flame out and then go stone dark. We watched as the guard stopped, took his time lighting another one of his cigarettes in the wind, then resumed his trip toward the central building.

Assad said, "My guess is he's coming up here to fuck with our heads."

I was hungry. The soldier entered the main building in a cloud of smoke. He threw his cigarette on the floor, crushed it beneath one of his boots. He sat in the only real chair in the room and looked at us through his dark glasses, a large man—huge actually. For some reason this hadn't occurred to me until we were alone with him in the small room.

He spoke to Assad at length.

Assad translated without enthusiasm. "He says he's going to be asking us questions, one by one. He's going to start with me and then use me as a translator. Mostly he wants to know about where we were last night and what we know about the body they found."

Pete said, "Mostly?"

The guard watched, expressionless.

"He says he has 'a few other matters' to raise as well."

I told Assad to ask when we could eat something. He did. The soldier responded.

Assad said, "He'll let us eat if he's satisfied with our answers."

I said, "*If?*"

Assad nodded. "Till then, everyone stays right here."

The soldier said something else to Assad—something that made Assad respond sharply. You didn't have to speak Arabic to know there was a dispute. The guard would say something with that smile of his and Assad would shake his head, no. I was unhappy with Assad and didn't believe it was a good idea to give the soldier any trouble.

"What's going on?" I asked.

"Just *wait*," Assad said.

They argued more and the soldier leaned to rest his elbows on his knees. Whatever he said was decisive, because Assad gave up. He looked at us, then looked away. He said, "Carolyn, this fellow wants you to stand up."

The soldier was still leaning forward—the whole scene mirrored back in warped refection by the lenses of his shades.

"All right," I said. " This is enough."

Carolyn said, "No, it's okay."

She stood. The guard watched. Through Assad, he told her to remove her dark glasses. She did. For the first time her composure wavered. There was something vulnerable about her without the dark glasses hiding her thoughts. Her light hair was pulled back, her head uncovered. Her blue eyes seemed to shine in the darkening room. Assad stared down at the floor. Pete had his eyes closed and was rubbing his forehead.

For a long time the soldier just looked. Finally he said something to Assad, never once directing his gaze away from Carolyn.

"He says give him the glasses." Carolyn did as she was told. The man leaned forward to take them. Assad said, "He wants to be able to see your eyes."

The wind was raging again and darkness had fallen. We were hungry and with the sun down it would soon grow cold inside the unheated hut. The guard had taken Assad into a side room to question him. We could hear their muted voices, the harsh and unsettling tones of spoken Arabic. I was sitting with Carolyn and Pete around the little table where we'd had tea that morning.

Pete said, "Look, there's got to be a way out of this place. A back door or through a window or something."

Carolyn said, "And then what? Run through a sandstorm to a bunch of cars that won't start? To drive off on a road that's covered with sand and leave Assad back here alone with that scary chap?"

Pete said, "There's the soldier's jeep."

I said, "How far do you suppose we'd get in an Arabic military vehicle, Pete? Besides, do you have the keys?"

Pete was rocking on his knees, looking at the table. He shook his head. "Well, we've got to do *something*. Just sitting here isn't making things any better and I sure as hell don't trust that soldier out there."

His slow unraveling made me anxious. I told him the best thing to do was just sit tight. We had no reason to mistrust the guards, or think this was anything other than routine questioning. I didn't believe it myself. But it sounded better than panicking. I suggested we simply wait until this thing played itself out.

"Wait? For what? Do you really think they're going to bring Desmond back safe and sound in the morning, tell us this was all just a crazy mix-up and send us off on our merry ways? Do we wait till they decide *I'm* a spy or that you're a killer and cut our goddamn hands off or some crazy shit like that?"

I said, "Come on, Pete."

He looked at me with an unpleasant smile in the half-light. He said, "You know, I can't even remember your fucking name, man."

I said, "I'm Martin. This is Carolyn. We're friends. It's a pleasure to meet you, Pete."

There was a strained silence.

Carolyn said she was hungry. Then she laughed. "I'd have eaten a larger breakfast had I known we'd be taken hostage this afternoon."

I was thinking about the food we'd brought in the desert box in the Land Cruiser. I thought maybe we could have Assad tell the guard we were hungry. Take a time out, a snack break from all the fun. I mentioned this. Carolyn shrugged. Pete wasn't listening. I said, "Also, I've got to go to the bathroom."

Pete stood up. "Look," he said, "I don't know what you people are doing out here. For all I know you *did* dump that body out there. I don't really give a fuck. But what I do know is that we're in serious trouble, all of us. As far as I'm concerned, it's that guy out there against us."

I said, "Pete—"

He said, "Just *listen* to me." You had to feel for the poor guy—a million miles from home, his pal marched off to God-knew-where. If the room had been large enough he would have been pacing. But he couldn't even do that.

He stared at me. "There's three of us here, man." He pointed at Carolyn. "Four if you count her and just one of him. I don't care what kind of weapons he has, we've got him outnumbered."

"Please, Pete," Carolyn said.

He waved his hand. "He's gonna finish talking to your friend out there and come through that door for one of us. When he does that, we're rushing him."

I said, "No we're not."

Pete said, "Yes, we are." We glared at each other, him standing, me sitting on one of the huge pillows beside the table.

Carolyn said, "I feel like I'm in the sort of movie I wouldn't care to see."

Pete was tall and athletic, had probably played some aggressive sport in college. Thinking that there was some action to take, however ill-conceived, made him feel better. One-hundred-percent all-American.

He smiled. "If I rush him, get him down on the ground, you and your friend will jump in. I *know* you will. Then we can go get the cars started and we'll be out of here."

Now I stood up. "Are you out of your fucking mind? If we do anything to that prick we really will be in trouble. All you'll manage to do is get yourself or one of us killed."

Carolyn said, "Boys...,"

We turned. Assad was coming in through the doorway looking at us. The guard stood behind wearing that scary grin of his.

Assad said, "What's all this?"

I looked steadily at Pete. "Nothing," I said. "We're just having a discussion. About food."

Assad looked weary. "He's done with me. I told him why we're here, but he doesn't seem very convinced. Seems to think we're all up to something together."

Pete nodded as if this confirmed what he'd been thinking all along. The guard was leaning against the doorjamb watching from behind his shades. He hadn't taken them off once and I got to wondering what was behind them—empty black orbs perhaps or just smaller versions of the dark shades? Then for some reason I got it into my head that he had eyes like a lizard, double-lidded, with vertical slits for pupils—some kind of desert-man, not human in all his parts. I found myself choking back dark laughter.

Behind me Carolyn said, "Doesn't this fellow ever get hungry?"

I said, "Or need to pee?"

Assad ignored us. "Look, he's going to talk to each of you now and I suggest you just tell the truth. Don't try to say anything fancy or clever. Just tell the entire fucking truth and we *might* get out of this in one piece."

I took this little speech to be aimed at me and was about to respond when a blur leapt before me. Assad was frozen in surprise as Pete landed a blow to the soldier's jaw, knocking the dark glasses askew. The soldier raised his truncheon in one practiced motion and struck Pete near the throat. There was the sound of a melon being dropped from a height, then another and a third. Pete dropped the way a fighter does, straight down, head first. Then the guard had his pistol drawn, pointing it at Assad. He said something in a low growling tone, then turned the gun on me.

He stepped toward me. The barrel of the pistol almost touched my face. I'd never had a gun pointed at me before. My nose and lips tingled; my mouth dried up and my knees felt watery. A twitch, a whim and my life was over. I stood there alive at the pleasure of another man, a strange soldier whose eyes were masked behind mirrored glasses. I had no idea what was going to happen next. I could think only of getting the gun out of my face.

Carolyn said, "Is he breathing?"

Assad said, "He bloody well doesn't deserve to be."

Carolyn had placed one of the pillows beneath Pete's head. She was leaning over him trying to figure out whether he was still alive. The wind was blowing as hard as it had been the evening before and the darkness outside was a velvety black shroud. A bulb burned in the anteroom of the mess hut, where the guard was drinking something from a canteen he'd brought in from his jeep. I wanted something to drink.

After the soldier had finally pulled the gun from my face, I'd felt a strange elation, a surge of gratitude that made me want to thank him or cry. He told me and Assad to tie Pete's hands behind his back with plastic cuffs. We did it. He watched us work, telling Assad he would shoot all of us as if there was another incident like that. Assad translated. We assured him there wouldn't be any more incidents. The soldier waved more cuffs in our faces. I could imagine us lined up beside Pete, hands lashed behind our backs, shot in the head one by one. Pete lay in a heap, motionless.

I said, "It smells like tea."

"What?" Carolyn said.

"What the guard's drinking. It smells like tea."

She said, "I don't think he's breathing."

"He's alive," I said. There were nasty trickles of blood from both his ears. "I think I saw him breathing."

Assad was sitting on one of the pillows, eyeing Pete as if he were a heap of laundry. "This idiot might well have handed us our death sentences," he said. "I'm tempted to finish him off myself."

The curtain separating the rooms parted. The guard stepped through, wiping his mouth. He nodded toward me. He said something to Assad.

Assad sighed, climbed to his feet.

I said, "Now what?"

Assad said, "It's your turn, mate."

We went through the curtains into the side room. A single chair was pushed up against the wall. The guard told me to sit. I could hear the wind behind the wall and imagined drifts of sand piling up, hiding things. If only the body had been hidden for another day, I thought. If only the soldiers hadn't happened by when they did. If only we had gone ahead into the desert or had just stayed back at home. Carolyn was in the mess room behind us all alone.

Circles had spread beneath Assad's eyes. His stomach growled. The guard lit another cigarette. Smoke curled from his nostrils. He spoke.

Assad said, "He'll be watching you close to make sure I'm not coaching you. Answer naturally. He's saying he wants to know what we're doing out here."

I described our business—that we were on a harmless scouting trip, something we did frequently. Two men and a married woman on a scouting trip. It sounded outlandish, the way the truth often does. The guard smiled as he listened. I said it was all very legal, we had all the necessary permits.

The guard responded—you could see he didn't believe a word we were saying.

"He doesn't care about our permits," Assad said. "He says he wants to know why we crossed over the border into Saudi."

"Saudi?" The word sounded exotic even as I said it. I shook my head for the guard's benefit. "We never crossed into Saudi. We know the limits, we stopped at this camp to *avoid* getting lost and going over the border accidentally."

Assad translated. The guard cut him off before he was done. Assad said: "He thinks you're lying."

"Well tell him I'm not."

Assad did. "He says they can prove we went over the border into Saudi."

I said it wasn't possible that he had proof because we hadn't gone there. I wondered why he wasn't asking anything about the body they had found. I wondered what he knew that we didn't. I said, "We never crossed over into Saudi. That's that. Maybe he's thinking of those guys, Pete and Desmond."

The guard was leaning against the wall watching me. He said something. Assad said, "He wants to know where you were last night."

I told him I was here, in the camp. Just like everyone else.

Assad spoke but the guard was shaking his head. He didn't mean that, he said, through Assad. I knew what he meant; he meant where was I, *precisely*.

"In my hut. Sound asleep."

The guard spoke. Assad looked at me. "He says that's funny. Because Hazem claims to have gone to your hut last night after lights out with some questions about the vehicle."

I said, "Then I must have been so soundly asleep that I didn't hear him knocking."

More translation.

Assad just smiled. "According to this fellow, Hazem let himself into your room. He claims the bed set was still made up and you were nowhere to be found."

I smiled tightly. "Then Hazem must be mistaken. Or lying."

"For God's sake, he was with me last night." Carolyn was standing in the doorway, watching. Her face was slightly drawn but she looked calm enough. She said, "He didn't cross the border and he didn't go out and kill anyone. We were together."

Assad looked at the floor. "You fools," he said, as if to himself. "You fucking bloody fools."

The guard understood. But he made us explain ourselves through Assad anyway—that we were not husband and wife, where her husband was. He enjoyed it, and when we were through he sat back in judgment to finish his cigarette. No one spoke. None of us looked at each other. We might not have been guilty of murder. But we were admitting to something that to him was nearly as bad. And we had come to this frontier, to his land, to carry out the deed.

Finally he spoke with Assad. He listened without looking up, as if had decided he was no longer involved in what was taking place. He said, "This man says he will expect us to make some kind of restitution."

I said, "Tell him to let us go so we can get some money."

Assad shook his head. "He doesn't want blood money." His raised his eyes to indicate Carolyn. "He wants her."

After a pause I said, "Tell him he can't have her."

"You don't think I already thought of that, mate?"

The soldier's hand was resting on his holstered gun. Carolyn was off to my side, her face was obscured in shadow.

I saw that Pete had been right. We were going to have to fight him—all three of us. It was us against him. I began to explain this to Assad with the guard standing right there in front of us.

Carolyn interrupted me. "Assad," she said, "I want you to ask this man something."

Assad nodded.

She said, "After we pay—after *I* pay—is he going to let us go?"

Assad said, "I'm not going to ask him that."

She told him to ask the question.

"We can't bargain with this man," I said. "We can't trust him, Carolyn."

She ignored me. She said, "I don't believe he's going to let us go unless he gets what he wants, Assad. I believe that we'll end up like that poor man out there."

There was a silence during which to think about this.

I said, "Carolyn, I'm not letting you go with him. I don't care whether we do get shot."

She exhaled sharply, a sound bordering on laughter. Her face was still hidden in shadow. "I do care," she said, "so please, Martin, shut up. Assad, ask him the question."

The guard made Assad and me sit back-to-back, then lashed our wrists together. We didn't speak or offer any resistance.

When he opened the door the wind roared and sand blew in. He slammed it shut and was gone with Carolyn. The plastic cuffs dug into my wrists. My hands went numb. I imagined them turning blue, then black like the night outside. I said, "We can't let this happen, Assad. We can't let this happen."

Assad said nothing.

I struggled until I couldn't struggle any more. My wrists felt bloody. After a while, I cried. I thought of Assad's words over and over: bloody fucking fools.

Outside the wind blew. More time passed and it began to get cold. I could no longer feel my hands. Assad and I were joined together like a single pathetic animal. He spoke only once in the night and I was shocked that when he did he woke me from a dark sleep. "I'm thirsty," he said.

The wind stopped some time before dawn, leaving a mournful stillness as it had the day before. I thought of having left Carolyn's hut that morning, going back to my own following the storm, now a memory from years ago. My shoulders were on fire. I tried to move my fingers but couldn't.

The first rays of sun came through the window, blood-colored, then full daylight broke, so bright it hurt my eyes. My mouth was parched, lips chapped and swollen. From where I sat I had a clear view into the other room where Pete lay. I could see the bottoms of his legs and his boots. He hadn't moved all night.

Soon it began to get hot. After what seemed to be a very long time I heard some sounds at the door, then I heard the door pushing open. The guard walked in with Carolyn behind him. At first they were just two dark figures, silhouetted before the blazing light. Then the guard scraped the door closed. I said Carolyn's name but she didn't answer, just hovered somewhere near the door.

A tool in the soldier's hand became a knife. After everything, I thought, this was what it came to: he was going to cut our throats right there in front of Carolyn.

He bent over us. When he did, I finally saw her. She was dressed as she had been the day before in her khakis and boots; her hair was pulled back again. Her hands were buried in her pockets, arms pressed tight against her sides. She looked at me for a moment, then away. A trickle of blood had dried at the corner of her mouth, and her jaw was deeply bruised. I felt as desolate as the desert outside.

The soldier cut the restraints from our wrists and stepped back.

Assad climbed to his feet. The guard spoke to Assad, who nodded his assent, then spoke to us without raising his eyes.

"He says we're free to go."

The soldier made us put Pete into his jeep, our second body in two days. But it was true—we were free to go. The man looked on as Assad reconnected the Land Cruiser's distributor and we got in. The desert was still, like a lake back home in the hot mid-summer. Assad sat rigidly behind the steering wheel as he directed the car away from camp, deep blood-toned marks on his wrists. Some time later we passed the spot where the body had lain the day before; later still we passed the tattered carcass of a camel resting against the side of a great mound of sand.

For a long time no one spoke. Then Carolyn asked what time it was. I looked at my watch, answered her.

"Somehow," she said, "it seems much later than that."

I agreed.

She wondered aloud what time it would be in London. Then she said she wondered where Barry, her husband, was right then. She doubted whether he would even be awake yet.

There was a silence.

I said, "We'll have to make them pay somehow. They have to pay."

After a long time Assad said, "Yes, Martin. We'll go directly to the authorities."

Carolyn had turned to the window. Her reflection hovered in the glass, a ghost gazing back at her.

She said, "It's strange in the morning, the desert, isn't it? It's really the strangest place."

I followed her gaze outside to the lonely landscape—sand, then blue sky, blank and pitiless, stretching upward before fading into something darker. We sat in silence on the long drive back to the city.

Samba

Heeber checked his watch again.
People hustled by—past the flickering tiki torches, on into the restaurant.
Laughter came from inside and music. Yet here he stood out front, alone
in the muggy night air. The valet, a hungry-looking kid in a baggy uni-
form, had twice approached. Heeber waved him off. He'd been warned
they were going to try to fleece him down here and had been on guard
since the move. They were all beggars of a sort, even the jewelry-wearing
ones passing him right now. Why else would they need a man like him
to run a power plant in their own damned country?

Another look at the watch. You expected this of locals. But his own
boss, Ellis, an American, had told him to be here at a certain time and here
he was. What got Heeber was that he'd wanted to go shopping, buy his
wife a souvenir (she lived stateside, he *missed* her). But Ellis had claimed
there wasn't time before dinner. This was earlier, at the golf course. Heeber had dutifully rushed home, changed and rushed here by taxi, only to
wait alone like a fool for over half an hour.

Tears stung his eyes. When the valet came toward him again, Heeber
growled that he didn't want any help.

Eight-and-a-half minutes later Ellis's Grand Cherokee pulled up, tiki
flames dancing in the windows. The valet hopped to the door. Ellis poured
himself out, followed by Luciano, a junior engineer—local personnel.
Both were beet-faced, laughing. They'd been off drinking somewhere.

Heeber raised a hand in greeting.

"Hi, Mr. Ellis," he said. "Isn't Simons coming?" Simons, Ellis's friend
from sales, had rounded out their foursome earlier.

Ellis walked a pace ahead of Luciano, palms upturned. His smile was
draining away. "Jesus Christ, Heeber. Look how you're dressed!"

Heeber looked. He was wearing shorts, a T-shirt, sandals. It was hot.
He looked back up.

"You're wearing a damn *Tigger* T-shirt, Heeber!"

"But you said casual, Mr. Ellis. I—"

"Casual, Heeber, not kindergarten. God *damn*." Ellis had cruel blue
eyes—pale, animal-like. Heeber often found it hard to look at the man.

Luciano leaned toward Ellis. "I do not believe they will allow him without the collar-shirt."

Ellis regarded Heeber for an unpleasant moment, then turned to the valet, snapping something off in Portuguese. The kid turned back in the direction from which he'd just come.

"I don't have to go in, Mr. Ellis. I mean, if there's a dress code or something."

"Oh, Christ, you're here already. Just wait."

Ellis himself wore black slacks and a golf shirt, hardly dressy. What got Heeber was that the T-shirt had been a gift from his four-year-old boy last Father's Day; he'd worn it out of homesickness, a way to feel closer to his wife and son.

The Grand Cherokee came rolling back up. Ellis opened the liftgate and rummaged around in back. He came out with a wadded up Hawaiian shirt.

"Here," he said. "Wear this." He threw it Heeber's way. "Consider it a gift."

The place was called a *churrascaria* and here you ate Brazilian-style. An army of waiters prowled the dining room with skewered meat, fish, chicken, sausage. Heeber liked his meat and potatoes but some of the food here was scary. Last time he'd seen a cart being pushed around with a fish on it the size of a man, toothy head still attached. You could lose your appetite. Crossing the dining room, Heeber was aware of eyes on him in the ridiculous shirt. The thing reeked of Ellis's musty cologne and stale sweat.

They were seated.

"Isn't Simons coming, Mr. Ellis?"

"He's coming, Heeber, he's coming." Ellis studied the menu without looking up. "He had a couple things to take care of, is all."

So. There was time for *Simons* to take care of things before dinner. Heeber made the mistake of glancing at Luciano, who wore his usual idiotic grin. At the golf course there had been no one else for Heeber to talk to and now the guy thought they were best friends.

"Did you find for your wife the gift you were looking for?" Luciano asked.

Heeber inspected the silverware in front of him. They used weird forks down here with only three prongs. "I'd rather not talk about it, Luciano."

"Answer the kid's question," Ellis snapped. The cold eyes were on him again. "Don't be an ass."

Luciano smiled awkwardly. "The souvenir? The CD of samba music?"

"I didn't get them yet," Heeber answered. "There wasn't enough time."

A waiter trundled up behind a bar cart, the way they did here. Ellis pointed at each man in turn. "*Caipirinha?*" he asked. "*Caipirinha? Três caipirinhas, por favor.*"

"Not for me," Heeber said. "Coca Lite, no ice?"

The waiter placed the warm can before him. Heeber wanted to make a joke about not drinking, as his wife had taught him. But Ellis sat motionless in his seat, jaw tensed, and the three of them watched in silence as the waiter sliced limes with a saw-toothed knife.

Simons materialized, rubbing his palms together.

"Everything's lined up for later, gents." He collapsed into the seat beside Ellis and looked across the table. "Jesus, Heeber. A*loha*! Check out the shirt on you."

"You think that's bad," Ellis said, "you should've seen what he had on earlier. Goddamn Tigger T-shirt! I had to give him that thing so we could get in."

"Tigger?"

"You know, the cartoon? 'The wonderful thing about Tiggers'—"

"—'is that Tiggers are wonderful things!'" Simons turned back to Heeber. "Grrrr!" he said.

Everyone, including Heeber, laughed. Then Ellis kept laughing, so hard that tears swam into his eyes. He had trouble ordering another round of drinks and Heeber thought: it's not *that* funny.

Waiters arrived bearing meat. Heeber was just starting in when Luciano came to life. "Ah, look," he said. "*Coraçao*! You must try here the *coraçao*. Is in all of Sao Paulo the best!"

"Hey, I got an idea," said Simons. "Let's try the *coraçao*."

They waved the waiter over. He carried a skewer studded with lumps of meat that looked like old blisters.

"Ah," Luciano said, "*espectacular*!" He kissed his bunched fingertips like a Frenchman. "This you must try, you must try."

The waiter bowed toward Heeber. Ellis nodded, grinning. He said something in Portuguese. Heeber smiled. "What are they, Mr. Ellis?"

"They're *chicken hearts*, Heeber." The waiter scraped half a dozen onto the plate. Heeber gripped the edge of the table as the things plopped down, God help him, like meaty droppings from some small carnivorous jungle beast.

They were crammed into a taxi. Simons to his right and Ellis up front were singing—drunkenly, off-key. "The Girl from Ipanema," a song Heeber had liked till now. On his left Luciano stared from behind a dumb grin. It was a workday tomorrow yet they were showing no signs of slowing down.

They entered an area of seedy buildings and garish light. Heeber squirmed and asked where they were going. No one answered. They sang another song. Finally the taxi stopped and deposited them in front of a bar with a blinking sign that read BLACK'S.

Heeber paused on the sidewalk as the others started for the steps.

"What are you waiting for?" Simons asked.

In the window glowed a neon girl with breasts like bananas. She blinked and her hips swayed from one side to the other, then back again.

Heeber forced a smile. "I think I'll just grab a taxi home, guys."

"Come on," said Simons, "we'll only be a couple hours."

Ellis observed in silence.

"No, that's okay, you guys go on." Heeber retreated a couple steps. "I have to work tomorrow."

There was some mumbling then Heeber heard Ellis say, distinctly, "Fuck him. Let him go." He and Simons headed for the door.

Luciano, a pained look in his eye, touched Heeber's elbow. "Mr. Heeber, please do come. Is fun to look. You do not have to *fack* any of the womans."

Heeber snatched his arm back. "I said I'm not *going*."

Of course, the cab had gone. Heeber stomped away with no clear destination in mind. Why had he agreed to dinner with Ellis and those guys in the first place? What was he thinking? What he didn't get was why Ellis hated him so much. He worked hard, he did what he was told. But that wasn't enough. You had to drink and chase women with the man.

Ellis!

Just the name made Heeber tremble. He kicked at some loose chunks of pavement. He spat.

That was when he heard a voice.

"Tudo bem?"

Heeber looked around, then down. Swaying along beside him, a little off to the side, was a boy—short-haired, barefoot, brown as a nut. It occurred to Heeber that this might not be the safest place to go for a walk. The boy cast a watchful eye down the street, where a patrol car waited at the curbside with green lights swimming overhead. Heeber let out a breath.

"English? Merican?"

"Go away," Heeber said. "I don't have any money."

"Ah, Merican. You need money? Change from dollars to *reais*?"

"No."

"Okay," the boy said. "How about souvenir. You like the souvenir?"

Heeber peered down at the kid. "Souvenirs?"

"Yeah, man. Souvenirs. Real nice, man. Nice deal!"

"Where?"

"Very near. *Tudo bem*, man. Real nice. Follow me, you."

Heeber glanced again in the direction of the patrol car. "Well," he said. "Okay, let's go."

The kid led him along for another block then down an alley. About half way down, right in the alley, they came to a storefront. The word *Bodega* was etched on the window and beneath that, *Umbanda*. The boy opened the door and beckoned Heeber to follow.

Potted palms sagged in the corners and oddly-shaped bird cages dangled overhead. Heeber bumped into a rack of outdated postcards. Behind the smell of dust and disuse lurked something else—something strange. Smoke, maybe, or incense. The boy vanished into a back room. A minute later, he returned with a woman in tow. She was taller than Heeber, dressed in a flowery African skirt, strong-looking and black as lava. A hemp blouse strained across her large breasts—a real, live Amazon, Heeber thought. And not bad looking either, though not his type.

"May I help you?" she asked in plain English.

"I guess so," Heeber said. "This boy, he said something about souvenirs?"

"We have souvenirs," she said. "We have works of art. Also we have animals: piranha fish or pet monkey. How about a tarot reading? Your fortune told? Ouija? Talk to the spirits?"

"Just souvenirs," Heeber said. "Something for my wife, you know, something really Brazilian. Maybe a woodcarving of a parrot, I saw one of those at the airport once, or some Brazilian music CDs, if you have them. I don't want any garbage that's gonna fall apart or not work, though."

The woman turned and left for the back room. The soles of her feet were pale and cracked like parched earth. The boy stared from behind the counter, and Heeber thought of the pet monkey the woman had offered.

She reemerged and to Heeber's surprise placed just what he'd been looking for on the countertop—a small wooden parrot like the one from the airport and a stack of several CDs. But Heeber knew that to show approval with these people was to ask for trouble.

"Do these even work?" He turned the CDs over. Beach scenes, pretty girls, and on each case a single word: *samba*. "I wanna hear them. Play them for me."

The woman wagged a finger in his face. "You remove wrapper, you bought CD."

He examined the wooden parrot. "This isn't even hand-carved." He shrugged. "So how much for everything?"

"Fifteen *reais*."

About five bucks—less than he was actually willing to spend. "Too much," he said.

The lady raised her shoulders. "Is late," she said. "Ten *reais*."

Heeber took care not to let them see how much money he had in his wallet.

"Would you like," she asked as he paid, "to cast a spell?"

"A what?"

"A spell. Good, bad. Perhaps to bring luck to a beloved one. Or to place the evil hex on some enemy for sweet revenge."

What was this mumbo jumbo? Heeber smiled. "Boy, do I ever know someone I'd like to put a hex on."

She made an accommodating gesture. "Costs only six *reais* to place the evil hex on an enemy. Is on special this week! Makes you feel real nice."

Two bucks. Now *there* was a bargain. "How do you do it?"

"First, you provide to me a personal item of the enemy. Then at midnight, I call on a demon to place the evil hex." She waved a hand. "Is all very simple. You don't even need to be here!"

"Well—" Heeber said with a laugh. "Not much chance of me getting my hands on—" He stopped short, fingering a button on the Hawaiian shirt. Ellis's cold blue eyes stared out at him from the dark. "Okay," he said. "What the heck!"

The African woman was confused as he passed the Hawaiian shirt over the counter. "But this is yours, no?"

"Trust me," he said. "Hex away."

She brought the shirt to her face and breathed in deeply. "Ahh," she said, her voice low and greedy like a man's. "Sweat. They *adore* sweat. Is very precious to them."

"Keep it," he said, surprised by his own bitterness. "Consider it a gift."

"I am supposed to warn you, mister. Exu of the Seven Crossroads, the dark being on whom you are calling, is restless and impulsive. Once called upon to perform evil he is not easily controlled." She shrugged. "Is just the fine print, though. Almost never there is trouble."

At first Heeber felt real nice. The souvenirs were a bargain and the hex a good gag—a couple of bucks to rid himself of the ugly shirt and have a laugh at Ellis's expense. But there was something about the African woman's warning that troubled him now. Riding home in the taxi he decided he'd been fleeced after all. Worse, he'd done it to himself! In front of his building he quibbled with the driver over the fare. Upstairs there were no messages from his wife. He put the souvenirs on the table beside the bed and tried calling her. The phone rang and rang and finally, feeling abandoned, he gave up.

In bed his heart raced. Ellis was in the room, insulting him, ordering him to do humiliating tasks: polish his golf balls, press his wrinkly slacks. The African woman was there too. She had thrown off her skirt and straddled Heeber, her great breasts in his face, the cracked soles of her feet beneath his calves. The bed rocked and groaned as they made love to pulsing jungle music. Ellis, squatting in the corner obscenely, wagged his tongue, taunting them. The music grew louder and more frantic. Heeber smelled blood and heard the panicked beating of wings. There were flashes of light, like bulbs exploding in his face. Someone cackled with laughter; someone else screamed.

Heeber sat up with a lurch. The salty meat, the Diet Coke—it had him all worked up! He warmed some milk in the kitchen but drinking it he had a thought. What if Ellis wanted the shirt back in the morning? It was like him. Heeber could imagine being teased mercilessly for not having the thing, a fresh torment. He poured his milk down the drain and began to pace. Now he wanted to find the African woman and demand the shirt back. For a long time he walked back and forth in his little kitchen, telling himself to calm down, cursing Ellis and the power the man had to make his life miserable.

He was late to work and poorly rested. He slipped past some locals gossiping at the *cafezinho* cart and ducked into his office. There was a rap on the door and Heeber looked up as if he'd been at the desk for hours.

"Mr. Heeber?" It was Daniela, the office secretary. "Are you unwell, sir?"

"I'm fine, thank you. I'm actually quite busy, however, so if you don't mind—"

"It is just that...have you not heard?"

Heeber's eyes narrowed. "Heard what?"

"Oh, my God. You have not heard!"

"Heard *what*?"

"About Mr. Ellis. That last night he is in the city assaulted by robbers?"

"You're kidding."

Her eyes grew round. "No, I am not. His car was, how you say, hijack?" She touched her temple. "When he is fighting they hit on him against the head with a pipe."

"Is he okay?"

"I believe he is alive, but no good."

Something scaly raced down Heeber's spine with icy feet. Was it possible?

"Simons from sales," he said, "and what's-his-name? Luciano. They were both with him last night. Were they involved?"

"No, sir. Mr. Ellis, he is all alone now going to home when he becomes attacked."

After work Heeber caught a cab to the American hospital. Ellis had a private suite overlooking a leafy park. Walking in, Heeber passed a little conference room by the door. *Ellis.* Even sick he got all the best perks.

The man himself lay beneath hospital sheets and was connected to a bank of machinery and a constellation of hanging bags. His eyes were ripe plums and a goose egg had grown on his forehead. At bedside stood his wife. Blonde-going-gray, pearls, a company wife.

She looked up as he came in. "Oh, hello," she said. "You work for Hank, don't you? Matt, right?"

"Rob," he said. "Rob, uh, Heeber." He cleared his throat. "How is he?"

She shook her head. "At first he seemed okay. He was joking, teasing everyone. You know how playful Hank is."

Heeber knew all about it.

"But then this afternoon he had an awful fit of some kind. The doctors says it's like that sometimes with a— closed head injury." Her hand came to her mouth. "Oh, we've never had trouble here before! Just last night Hank had dinner with friends then went back to the office to work late. You know how hard he works."

"Yes." Heeber cleared his throat again. "Hard."

Ellis's bruised eyelids fluttered. "Claire? Are you here?"

"I'm here."

"Don't leave," he said, "okay? Who were you talking to?"

"Your friend, dear. David Heeber, from the office."

The feral eyes turned toward him. "Heeber? What the hell are you doing here?"

Sweat broke out on Heeber's forehead. "I came to visit when I heard about your—accident, Mr. Ellis."

"Accident? Christ, this was no accident. Just what the hell is going on here? Why are my eyes black? Where's all my money? Heeber, what the *hell* did you do with the goddamned shirt?"

Ellis's wife looked stricken.

"Heeber, do you hear me? I want it, bring it to the office or to the golf course if you have to."

"You see," she whispered, "he says crazy things."

"Like all mixed up," Heeber said.

"Claire, are you here? Don't leave me!"

"I'm not leaving, dear. I'm right here."

"Heeber," he said. "*Heeber!*"

"Yes?"

Ellis climbed up on his elbows. "Listen to me, you—" Suddenly his head jerked back and veins popped out like hard blue cables in his neck. He made strangling noises; spit sizzled across his lips. The machines chirped like startled birds as Ellis bucked and kicked. The wife gasped. A doctor rushed in, a nurse. Heeber fled.

He muttered his address to the cab driver then stared out at the hellish cityscape. What was going on? It was a gag, a harmless joke! True, if anyone deserved a hex it was Ellis. He was a hateful, lying man. But Heeber hadn't imagined him jerking around like that in bed. And what, by the way, was *he* doing? Rob Heeber, a decent, God-fearing American, believing in the hocus pocus of foreign people!

On the dashboard stood a cloth doll clutching feathers and voodoo beads, a little pagan shrine right there in the cab. It was this place, Heeber thought, these people. They were to blame! Ellis was to blame! Forget the hex, Heeber thought. Ellis was American—he was *corporate*. This made his mugging newsworthy. The African woman would see the news, put two and two together, figure out who Heeber was. She and the boy would track him down, blackmail him and ruin him at work.

He rocked in his seat; he groaned.

The driver glanced at the rearview mirror. "You okay, mister?"

"Just drive," Heeber said. And then: "Wait a minute. Do you know where Black's is?"

The driver grinned. "Ah, Black's."

"Take me there."

"Is real nice, Black's. *Real* nice."

"Just shut up and drive!"

He wandered the streets. Nothing ever looked the same way twice in this city, as if the place shifted and changed shape nightly. He walked up dead alleys. Where was the little boy now that Heeber needed him? People would take notice—a white man with money walking these streets alone. He began to sweat. He stopped and looked around, walked a few more blocks. He was ready to give up when he stumbled into an alley. Halfway down was the sign: *Bodega. Umbanda.* Was it the woman's name?

The place looked different this time, shimmering and hot, lit by a hundred candles. The boy, perched in his place behind the counter, gawked, a wicked imp. The woman listened to Heeber's story with a look on her face like *he* was the weird one here.

She shook her head. "You ask for the evil hex. The evil hex works. But now you ask me to undo it?"

"That's right, reverse it. Call the whole thing off. It was just a crazy mix-up."

"Is not so easy. Exu of the Seven Crossroads is very, very powerful. Didn't I warn you? Didn't I tell you that when you ask for evil to be done, you—"

"Yes, yes, you warned me! I don't want to hear it again!"

She stroked her chin and Heeber found himself staring at the awesome swell of her breasts, his dream coming back now, embarrassing and arousing at the same time. The woman said something to the boy in Portuguese; he grinned at Heeber and replied at length.

The woman turned back. "There is one possibility. To reverse the hex, first you must retake possession of the shirt, buy it back from me. Then at midnight in your home—it must be your own home and it must be at midnight—you must destroy the shirt by fire as an offering."

"You mean burn it? I live in an apartment. I can't set a fire there."

"You ask me to undo the hex. If you're going to tie my hands..."

"All right, all right, skip it." He took out his wallet. "How much to buy back the shirt?"

"Is one hundred reais."

"One *hundred*? That's almost forty dollars!"

"To reverse hex is a different story. Costs a little more."

"So that's how it works, huh?" Heeber bitterly counted out the bills. "You charge two dollars to *place* an evil hex but *forty* to take it back. Pretty clever."

The woman showed her palms. "Is the going rate, mister."

The little boy disappeared into the back room. A minute later he scampered back with the horrid shirt.

At the door, Heeber turned. "What if it won't burn?"

"Don't worry, is polyester. It should burn real nice."

Heeber downed three warm milks, one right after another. Then he climbed a chair to remove the battery from the smoke alarm on the kitchen ceiling. He opened the windows in the living room. In the bedroom the wooden parrot stared at him with an evil countenance. He slapped the thing from the nightstand. The bathroom window was jammed shut. Heeber seriously considered breaking the glass, going so far as to wrap his fist in a towel. But what if the neighbors heard? In the end he used a heavy book to pound the jamb until the window gave. Damp tropical air flooded the little bathroom. Now he waited.

Music from the next apartment bled through the cheaply constructed walls. Heavy on the drums, tribal and crazy. It played on and on. When his watch read five till midnight, Heeber placed the shirt in the sink basin. Then he realized that that he had no fire—he didn't smoke, he didn't have a lighter. He scrambled to the kitchen and opened empty drawers looking for matches that weren't there. How much time did he have? The African woman hadn't said. He panicked, then looked at the stove. He rolled up a paper towel, held it to the hot coils.

Back in the bathroom he touched the flame to the shirt. The nasty thing began to move in the sink, squirming, alive with tiny worms of fire. Soon tarry smoke filled the bathroom. He realized that it had been a mistake to open the windows—the neighbors would smell the smoke. The shirt writhed like something dying in the sink basin.

When he left the bathroom the phone was ringing. It was his wife.

"Rob, is that you?

"I've been trying to call all week," he said.

"Rob? Are you okay?"

"I'm fine."

"Are you sure? You sound strange."

"Strange? Why would I sound strange?" A laugh escaped from high in his throat. "I live in a third world hellhole full of insane people where you can find a witchdoctor on every corner but you can't eat dinner in a fucking T-shirt. I have a boss that treats me like crap. I hate my job. I hate my life. How could any of that possibly *bother* me?"

"Rob, you're scaring me. You're not making any sense."

He paused. "It's been a strange couple of days. I miss you."

"I miss you, too."

"It's this place," he said. "I hate it."

"Poor Rob."

"I hate it, I hate it!"

He skipped work next morning and went straight to the hospital. Stepping from the elevator, he ran into Simons. The man's face sagged like loose clothing. "Hey, Rob," he said quietly, "how's it going, buddy?"

Rob? Buddy? Since when was Simons treating him so nice? Heeber asked how Ellis was doing.

Simons shook his head. "Not so good."

Well, there it was. He'd been fleeced again.

"It's the damndest thing, isn't it?" Simons asked. "How everything can change overnight?"

In the room the wife stood beside the bed. Now a tube ran from Ellis's nose to the back of his head. He seemed to be asleep.

"You're back," Ellis's wife said. "He was asking about you."

"About me?"

"He's so close to the men who work for him."

The doctor entered. He was tall and brown, Brazilian-looking, yet spoke English like an American. He nodded at Heeber without curiosity and told the wife he wanted to speak to her. Heeber said he would leave.

"No," she said, "stay. I'm sure Hank would want you to."

They followed the doctor to the sitting area. He described Ellis's condition and how it had worsened overnight; the tube in his head was called a shunt, he said, and it was draining fluid from the brain. The wife covered her mouth as the doctor spoke of things Heeber knew nothing about: left temporal seizure disorder, epileptic fugue, postictal disorientation.

The shunt was only a short-term fix, which was why they were recommending an operation. It was not exactly a lobotomy, the doctor explained—just a procedure intended to stop the seizures long enough to fly Ellis home safely. Head injuries were like that, he said. They could take a turn for better or worse at any time. For now, the doctor said, the important thing was to keep him calm and avoid upsetting him. He did, however, warn that there was a chance the procedure would fail.

"Fail?" the wife said. "Oh, my."

"I'm confident everything will turn out well. You might want to call any friends or relatives in the area, however. The nurse will let you use the telephone in my office."

She thanked the doctor and turned to touch Heeber's hand. "Will you stay while I make a few calls? You've been such a help."

Heeber agreed and she left.

"This operation," Heeber said, "you really have to do it? There's no other way?"

"It's very likely that he wouldn't survive a flight home without it."

"Tell me the truth, Doc. Is it risky?"

The doctor considered the question. "Quite," he said.

The doctor left and Heeber returned to the bed alone. Ellis was awake now, stirring. "Claire? Is that you?"

"No. It's me."

The eyes rolled toward Heeber. They were different now, strawberry-speckled, weak. No ice there, no cruelty. Ellis was scared, you could see it in his eyes. "Heeber? Where's Claire?"

"She had to go make some phone calls."

"You won't leave till she gets back, will you?"

Heeber promised to stay.

Ellis had become old overnight. He was shriveled, unmanned by injury. The word *chickenhearted* came to mind. He did, however, seem much nicer this way.

"Why did Claire have to go make *phone* calls, Heeber?"

"Because," he said, "they're going to do an operation on you."

"An operation?"

"Yes. On your brain. They're going cut your head open and do a lobotomy on it."

"A lobotomy?" Ellis clutched Heeber's hand. "On my *brain*?"

"The left lobe part," Heeber said.

"The left lobe? An operation? Is it dangerous?"

Heeber leaned over, close enough to feel Ellis's warm breath—close enough to kiss the man. "*Quite*," he said finally.

The eyes grew wide with fear; Ellis actually began to sob.

"Don't worry," Heeber said, wrenching his hand free in disgust. "I'll be here with you the whole time."

Johnson, the Driver

I had been working in the Sandton office for over a year when my boss called me into his office, never a good thing. I found Quinn slouched in his leather chair, index fingers pressed to his lips in the pensive attitude he assumed when plotting office coups. Quinn liked me. This meant that I was often called on to do his dirty work.

"Question for you, Harris."

"Sir," I said. Quinn fancied himself a soldierly man and I knew how he liked a conversation to go.

"Tell me. What do you know about Johnson what's-his-name, the old boy down in the motor pool?"

"Johnson, the driver?"

He squirmed in his seat. He didn't like to hear a question answered with another question but I wasn't sure what he was fishing for.

"The chief driver. *My* driver, Harris."

"He was here before I arrived," I said. "As far as I know he's been with us since we reopened shop down here."

The index fingers were back on the lips again.

"Never had an accident. He's reliable, never late. Top notch, sir. Nice fellow, too." What else was there to know? The man was a driver. "Is there some problem?"

"The problem, Harris, is that he's been stealing from me."

"Stealing?"

Quinn's expression registered that I had asked yet another question.

"Yes, Harris, stealing. Taking things. From the limo. I haven't personally missed anything yet but my wife had a pocketbook disappear last week and a few other items. My youngest daughter had a bracelet go missing."

Two months earlier Quinn's family had joined him from the States, a touchy issue. Among senior staff it was an open secret that before their arrival Quinn had kept a mistress in the city. The less cynical staffers viewed his family's sudden appearance as evidence that Quinn was mending his ways. The rest of us figured he'd gotten the expatriate wife's ultimatum: move me or lose me. Quinn was understandably concerned for his family's safety and oddly secretive about them.

Still, a driver stealing? It seemed unlikely. "The drivers are pretty reliable, sir, Johnson especially. You're sure it can't be something else?"

"The items were all last seen in the limo, Harris. You don't have to be Sherlock Holmes to see a pattern."

"No, sir."

Quinn climbed to his feet. The window behind his desk commanded views of glass buildings and the business district's treetops. Beyond the district's walls were dun-colored African expanses. He came around the desk to stand in front of me.

"I want you to let him go, Harris, fire the man." He studied my careful lack of expression. "It's time for new blood in the motor pool, anyway. You practically said so yourself. He's been here forever, this driver. I mean, people are gonna start to wonder who's running the show down here!"

"A reliable driver is hard to find, sir. Don't you think he at least deserves a chance to explain himself?"

"I appreciate what you're saying, Harris. Believe me, I do. But stealing is something I will not tolerate. It's something I nip in the bud."

"*If* he's stealing, sir."

Quinn's face clouded over. "We're talking about my daughter's bracelet, here, Harris. Or would you care to offer another theory?"

"No, sir. No theories from me."

Quinn smiled. "Good man, Harris. I know you have a way with the locals. That's why I want you to be the one to deliver the news—coming from you, it won't be such a letdown for the old boy."

By which Quinn meant that that he didn't have the stomach to accuse a man to his face and fire him himself.

"That's thoughtful of you, sir."

He clapped my shoulder, a dismissal. "I knew I could count on you. That's why I turn to you when something needs doing."

Quinn's tone was hearty—friendly, even—and I knew I was being warned.

I made some trivial calls, I had a long lunch in Sandton. But when I got back I knew I had to get the disagreeable task over with. I buzzed Fiona, my secretary, and told her to call Johnson upstairs. This would distress him. Drivers waited out front when one of us needed a ride and were never invited upstairs. But I thought it would be better than firing him in front of the other workers in the motor pool.

A rap came at my door and I told Johnson to come in. He was a small man, slim, with steel wool for hair and yellowish eyes. His face had flat African features, the skin cragged and furrowed like the dark earth of the Lowveld in wet season. He was one of those old men who took an unimportant job very seriously; his neatly pressed trousers and anxious expression made me feel even worse for what I was about to do.

"Johnson, how are things going?" This sounded stupid, even to my ears. "You know, I mean—on the job?"

"The job, sir?" Johnson asked.

"Have you been having problems? Is there something you feel that you'd like to share with us?"

"Share with you, sir?"

"We don't answer questions with questions around here, Johnson," I said. "We're looking into performance issues among some of the local employees."

In his eyes I saw the resignation of a decent man accustomed to the treachery of others. "Am I in trouble for something I've done, sir?"

"Why don't you tell me, Johnson? Are you?"

"Mister Mike?" It was a manner of address common among the indigenous people and I despised it for its blatant obsequiousness. "I do my job. Have I done a bad job, sir?"

"Johnson, we run a serious business around here, an *important* business—a business based on mutual trust and openness. We don't tolerate certain things among the staff, Johnson—not even the *appearance* of certain things—and one of those is stealing."

The old man looked as if I'd spat. I'd been dreading the inevitable groveling but what happened next surprised me. Johnson drew himself upright and said, "I have never stolen anything in my life." He said this with dignity and in a tone that had the effect of making me feel like a small and peevish man. "Don't call me a thief, sir."

"I haven't called you a thief, Johnson. I said I'm investigating 'performance issues.'"

"If people have complaints they should come forward and ask me directly."

Johnson's job perhaps saved him from poverty and it took guts for him to stand up to me. I had called him into my office to fire him but now found myself admiring the man. The fact that I agreed entirely with his point didn't help matters much. I sighed. I decided then to stall for time.

"Johnson, *I'm* not accusing you of anything. I'm just looking into certain issues, as I said. I want you to know, however, that I am doing this."

He hesitated. "I'm not a thief, Mister Mike."

He turned to leave and I thought of a question I should have asked earlier. "Johnson. One other thing." He stopped. "Have you made any unusual trips in the last few weeks? That is, in company cars?"

He watched me unhappily, not sure what I was aiming for. "Unusual trips? I don't think so, sir."

"Anything you can think of," I said, "anywhere out of the ordinary? Think carefully."

He thought. He seemed conflicted and for a moment it looked like he maybe had something to admit. But then shook his head.

"No, Mr. Mike. Nothing unusual."

Our office was a branch of the heavy applications division of Mason Worldwide, and our job was to push specially clad military vehicles to the South African government. The account was important to us and though my college degree said mechanical engineer on it, I knew that I was basically a salesman. There was a major presentation coming up with an important colonel and a few deputy ministers, I had a lot of work to do and now Quinn was saddling me with this unrelated job.

But as Johnson left my office, straight-backed and without a second look in my direction, I got a feeling that something funny was going on. By the end of the day I'd gotten no work done, and neither had I fired the man. I sent Fiona home. When I was sure she had left, I made a call to the motor pool from her phone, then headed downstairs to the garage.

It was the first week in May, early fall down here, but still warm and sunny. I crossed the unpaved lot to the garage, orange dust painting my shoes and the cuffs of my pants. The main building on our installation was an American glass-and-steel structure. Lesser operations—shipping and receiving, the motorpool—were run out of older buildings. These were manned by local blacks, men and women happy to walk an hour or two each day to work for subsistence wages. A white face down here was as rare as a black one in the executive offices and could only mean trouble for the locals. I was sure Quinn had never set foot in the motor pool.

I entered the bare front office of the garage. An airconditioner wheezed in the window. It smelled musty. The receptionist regarded me with alarm—no good came of a white man in a suit showing up.

"Good afternoon," I said. "Or evening, I mean. You're working late tonight, aren't you?"

"I'm sorry, sir," she said.

"No, I didn't mean you're working *too* late, I meant—" The woman's eyes grew even larger, and I could see my American weirdness and unpredictability were scaring her. "Never mind. I called earlier. I was hoping to take a look at the drivers' logs for the last two months."

"I remember, sir."

She led me down a corridor and left me alone in a windowless back room. The drivers were required to log each trip they made and record an address and a phone number beside it. Beneath a bare bulb, I skimmed for entries with Johnson's name. Most were familiar destinations, places any one of us might have done business. But as I had suspected, I found a handful of strange entries. Each stop listed the same address and telephone number that I didn't recognize.

I put the logs away. I took out my private cell phone and dialed the number listed with the entries, wanting to be sure. There were several rings before a woman's voice—a voice I didn't know—answered. "Hello? *Hello*? Who is this, please?"

So, I thought, hanging up. I put the phone back in my pocket. Johnson the driver had a secret after all.

I stopped at Fiona's apartment on my way home and after drinks we sat on her couch and watched the local news. It carried the usual gloom and doom. Workers in Johannesburg were threatening a transit strike and there had been more riots. A man had been beaten by other blacks outside of the Soweto shanty town and then "necklaced"—a tire soaked with gasoline had been hung around his neck and set on fire.

Next was a follow-up story about the Hyundai executive who'd been dragged from his car ten days earlier and shot in the head. Carjacking wasn't unusual in itself. But the fact that it had happened to a high-level businessman, an expat, within sight of Sandton's gates and in broad daylight, was unwelcome news indeed. The suburb was surrounded by walls and insulated with money, and usually Johannesburg might as well have been on another planet. The murder was a reminder of how vulnerable we really were.

"*Must* we listen to this depressing rot?" Fiona asked.

I clicked the TV off.

"You're quiet tonight."

"You know...," I said. "Work."

She laughed softly and said under her breath: "*Americans*."

"Fiona, do you know anything about the drivers at work?"

"The drivers?" she asked. "What?"

"I was wondering what you know about the people who work for us—the blacks, like the drivers?"

"I'm not *that* local," she said.

"I didn't mean that. I meant what do you *know* about them? Does anyone know about their personal lives? Johnson, for instance. Does he have kids? A wife?"

"Why would I know? Why would I *want* to know?"

"It seems unnatural," I said. "We work with these people and yet know nothing about them. Not a single thing. At home it would be different."

"Would it? You Americans. Always comparing everyone and everything with 'home.' Unfavorably, of course. It's not like my life revolves around the local blacks. Nor does yours, I might add." She sipped wine. "What is all this about drivers? Is there some problem?"

"No problem," I said. "I was just wondering what you know about them."

"I know they have damned fine jobs, for coloreds—for '*locals*,'" she corrected, remembering my American discomfort at the other word. "If you want to know something, Mister Mike, why not ask the blacks yourself? See how comfortable *they* are with your questions."

Later, I was dressing to leave for my place. "Let's not mention what we talked about tonight, Fiona," I said. "You know, about the driver? Not at work."

"Hah!" she said, drawing the sheets to her throat. "As if *I* would mention anything there." For we too had our secrets.

The next morning Fiona told me in her professional way that Quinn wanted to see me. I went to his office.

"Good morning, Harris. And a nice morning it is."

"Yes, sir. Not nearly as warm as yesterday, though."

"Not nearly. Fall's arrived. Harris, I couldn't help noticing that it was Johnson who picked me up this morning at the condo."

"Yes, sir."

"This ain't home, Mike. We don't have to give a driver two weeks notice before canning him. Or did I miss some new directive about blacks from the Ministry of Culture?"

"I haven't fired him yet, sir. I did give him a warning, though ."

"A warning? I didn't ask you to give a goddamn warning, Harris. I told you to fire the son-of-a-bitch."

I moved closer to Quinn's desk. "Hear me out, sir. I've been doing a little investigating and I think I might be on to something interesting about Johnson."

"Interesting? About him? Like what?"

"I'm not quite prepared to say, sir. But I will say that I am looking into other things. Possibly more serious issues."

Quinn was listening now. His head was tilted like a large, furry animal hearing a funny noise. "Serious? Let's not waste time with this, Harris. I don't wanna go on some wild goose chase. I just want the old guy fired."

"Of course, sir. But there's this presentation coming up at Gerotech and I'm not sure it's such good idea to use a new driver for that. Pretoria can be dangerous and Johnson knows his way around up there."

"Well." Quinn nodded vaguely. "I suppose, in light of recent events. That poor Korean bastard in town." He chuckled.

"It's what I was thinking, sir." I leaned closer in an attitude of conspiracy. "And *I* think we should give the driver a little more time, let out a little more noose for him to play with."

"Noose?"

"I'm just saying, sir, let's get what we can out of the man. All due respect, but if he's a thief, he should get what he's got coming. He'll hang himself eventually."

Quinn's index fingers were pressed to his lips. His eyes had narrowed. "You seem a little gung-ho all of a sudden."

"It's just that I can't stand a liar, sir." And I promised to speak with Johnson again that afternoon.

Pretoria is a relatively short distance from Sandton but it can seem like a long way. Once you leave the greater Johannesburg area, with its sprawl of white suburbs and black shantytowns, the Pretoria highway slices through scrubland and into the mountains of the Highveld beyond. Broken macadam forms huge tooth-like serrations on the road's edge most of the way, a giant savage smile. Dotting the landscape here and there are little lean-to villages, lawless and desperate places, one-time mining towns where no white men show their faces.

We set out for Pretoria on this highway first thing next morning, Quinn and I in the back seat, Johnson up front driving. A sea of zinc roofs reflected sunlight from the shantytowns as we headed north. At this early hour, men and women, all blacks, could be seen patiently walking the roadside on their way to downtown jobs.

I turned on my laptop to brief Quinn on our presentation. In front, Johnson carefully ignored us both.

An hour later we were being passed through the first set of gates at Gerotech, a rambling military installation tucked into the rugged foot-hills of the Mageliesburg Mountains. The place was a military playground, a Disneyland of war games. You could see why Paul Kruger had chosen to launch the Boer War from this forbidding region, why the Apartheid-era government was rumored to have hidden its nuclear bomb somewhere on these very grounds.

Colonel Pym and his staff of blond giants were waiting for us in front of the main office facility. He shook my hand then tossed an arm over Quinn's shoulders. Johnson, of course, might have been a small, black mongrel. I looked over my shoulder as we walked through the heavy doors and caught the man glancing after me. He quickly turned his attention back to the limo and began tinkering under its hood as we entered the main building.

We gave our presentation and then lunched: loud jokes, steaks and beer, Cuban cigars, business as usual. According to plan, I kept glancing at my watch and leaning toward Quinn to remind him, in a voice just loud enough for the South Africans to overhear, that we had a late-after-noon conference call with the States. We shook hands with Pym and his staff at four thirty in the afternoon and then stepped back outside.

Mountain light had set the edges of things on fire. Johnson seemed not to have moved all day from his spot beside the car. As he drove around to pick us up, I stood facing the autumnal wind. It swept uphill from the south, as if from Antarctica itself, fresh and fierce, making the chaparral and scrub trees shiver like feeling things on the stepped hills below.

The Pretoria highway was never heavily traveled; late in the after-noon it was downright desolate. The temperature had cooled over the last couple days but the sun glared down hard on the open spaces on either side of the road as we descended in the direction of the city.

From one of the unnamed roads servicing distant villages to the west a battered van pulled out in front of us. It seemed ancient, like any car you saw in black areas. It crawled along. Quinn looked up from a sheaf of papers to ask what the hell was going on.

"This van, sir," Johnson said. "It's blocking our way."

"Well, pass it."

"Yes sir," Johnson said.

Overtaking to the right was out of the question because the shoulder would gnaw the tire plies to strings. Johnson swung into the oncoming lane and stepped on the pedal but the van sped up with us. Johnson upped the gas a little more. The rattle-trap van, with its dented sides and unpainted fenders, shuddered but kept up surprisingly well.

"What the hell?" Quinn asked.

Suddenly, a second van appeared less than two hundred yards in front of us in the oncoming lane. Johnson had to slam the brakes and swerve back behind the first van. Quinn fell heavily against me, papers scattered to the floor. In front of us the red van slowed again, forcing us to slow with it. I realized then that the second van had swung a U-turn in the middle of the road and come up behind us. We were being forced to stop on the side of the road.

A minute later a tall black man was rapping the window with huge knobby knuckles. A second man was motioning us out of the car. Both wore bandanas pulled over their mouths and noses.

Quinn looked at me. His tongue ran along his lips but didn't speak. The tall man rapped the window again, harder this time. He looked in with menacing yellow eyes.

"Now what?" Quinn asked nervously.

"I think we better do what they say."

The carjackers were dressed in dark disco shirts and sandals made from old tire treads. I'd forgotten how much cooler it was today than the day before and standing in the long shadows at the side of the road I shivered. Johnson had gotten out and was talking stridently with one of the men in Zulu. Fingers were jabbed at the air, shouts made. Quinn observed the proceedings in grave silence. Then a third man emerged from the van in front of us. This one held a small revolver our way. Quinn paled. He was moon- faced and scared, a slow fat child before the spidery men confronting us.

From the corner of my eye I saw Johnson moving. He had returned to the car and was emerging now with a pipe. He swung it at the two unarmed men who backed away. He spun then on the one with the gun.

"Johnson!" I called.

The gunman seemed shocked, rooted in his place, staring at the little old man who was swinging the pipe, cricket-style, at him. Johnson was shouting for us to get back in the car as he moved forward.

"I think we should do what *he* says!" Quinn cried.

I followed as he ducked into the backseat. There we lay together like frightened children among the spilled papers. When I peeked up I saw that Johnson was climbing quickly back into the car. He didn't speak. He slammed the door behind him and, racing the engine, spun the steering wheel with short powerful arms and the limo shot out from between the vans and back onto the road.

We drove fast and in silence. The vans remained where they were behind us. Of the men there was no sign. It was Johnson who spoke first, after nearly five minutes. He shook his head, intent on the road, muttering, "Very bad. Very bad."

Quinn was smiling, sort of. He was playing with one of the toy armored vehicles on his desk, pushing it back and forth, back and forth. He looked like someone who'd thrown up half an hour earlier then splashed water on his face to pull himself together.

"It's good," he said, "that we kept our heads out there and didn't call the police."

"The so-*called* police."

He pushed the little 4x4 up to the picture of himself in dress blues, made the toy truck do a reverse turn.

"This doesn't go beyond us, you understand. Ever. No need to get an incident like this in the news. Bad PR."

"The worst." I waited for a few moments. His eyes remained fixed on the toy truck. "Sir, about Johnson, the driver? Should I, you know, give him the bad news now? Or later?"

His eyes came up from the toy. His eyebrows gathered above his nose as I thought they would. "I'm not sure what you're talking about, Harris."

"Johnson, his—performance."

Quinn went back to the toy truck. "Jesus, Harris. The man practically saved our lives out there."

"Well, sir. The stealing. The lying."

He shook his head, almost sadly. "You never know what you're made of till you're tested, Harris." He glanced at me, back down. "Maybe you never know. We can give him a second chance, I think."

As I left the office, I noticed that he had returned to playing with the little armored truck, a toy given to him by some general or another.

I got to the motor pool just as a battered white car was pulling in. Johnson came forward with a doubtful look on his face. The car parked and a tall black man unfolded himself from the driver's seat. He wore the sort of hairstyle popular at home twenty years ago. His smile was as wide as Johnson's frown was deep. The tall man extended his hand for me to shake and I felt the knobby knuckles in my grip.

"Stop smiling." Johnson said in English.

The man obeyed his uncle and the grin disappeared. But as I counted out the bills for him and his pals and handed them over, the smile was back. The nephew left with a wave and a low guttural laugh, a deep, happy laugh.

Johnson hadn't said a word and I wasn't going to ask him to. He looked at me seriously and then I turned to go.

"A bad thing, this theater."

I turned back to him. "It's not so good," I said. "But sometimes you have to protect yourself." I slapped his shoulder lightly and then turned to leave him to polish fenders and clean windows or do whatever it was he did with his life.

From behind, as I left, he thanked me.

"Never could *stand* the man," Fiona said. We were watching the sunset from her balcony. "But how did you know?"

"I just guessed. The trip logs tipped me off. When I made the phone call...you know, I was certain about it then."

"Mighty sure of yourself, I'd say."

I turned the stem of my wine glass. "You should have seen Quinn's face when he saw the gun."

Fiona sipped her wine. "So the poor man was covering up for driving him to visit his *mistress*? Yuck."

"The only lie he told was to me. But I knew he was no thief." I smiled slightly, shook my head. "He just didn't want to let me know where he was taking the Big Boss."

"But Quinn, the bastard, was afraid he'd talk anyway."

"It just didn't seem fair to me, you know. To *fire* the man?"

Fiona smiled. "Fair," she said and then she laughed. She repeated the word, *fair*. "My American!"

Road Train

Reese got the idea sitting at a bar in Freemantle, just south of Perth, in the furthermost reaches of Western Australia. It was late afternoon, a private catamaran the length of a football field was putting out of port, and the sun had begun its descent over the sea. In an expansive mood, Reese ordered another pint and told the bartender he was a journalist.

"That so?" The kid smiled, showing a mouthful of piano keys. "So what's brought you to Oz, then? More than Victoria Bitters and meat pies, I reckon."

Reese sipped his beer and told the thumbnail version of his story: he'd come to Australia with a cushy job for a well-known American magazine to cover the Olympics. He'd fallen in love with Australia, took a gamble, quit his job. Since then he'd been earning his keep as a stringer out of Sydney, covering all things Australian for anyone willing to pay.

"Stringer?" the kid said: *stringah.*

"A freelance writer, you know, a hired pen. I have contacts at papers and magazines—editors, other writers. I see an interesting story, I write about it."

"Yeah?" the bartender said. "You make a living at that?"

Reese did, a good one. For his articles he had hunted sharks off the Great Barrier Reef, hang glided in the Blue Mountains and bushwalked through the Valley of the Winds in Kata Tjuta near Uluru. In fact, Reese explained, he had just finished filing a feature from Perth on Australia's effort to win back the World Cup. He'd decided to shoot down to Freo for the afternoon and have a look.

The kid had perched a foot on the sink behind the bar. "A sporting man, eh? Sounds pretty exciting."

"Well," Reese said, "every job has its exciting side."

A bar-side printer spat paper. The bartender grinned as he tore it from the machine and read an order. "Not this job, mate, I'll say that."

Reese set to work on his beer. He was almost ready for another when a hand touched his shoulder; beside him, as if from nowhere, had appeared a powerfully-built and very short man.

"Mate, I hear you saying you was a journo?"

Yes, Reese admitted, he had.

"Fascinating," the man said. He took the stool beside Reese. "Listen, I got a story for you."

"Oh, yeah?" An occupational hazard: people always had a story. This fellow had a Buddha-like belly and a snarl of frizzy black hair bound up in a ponytail. By appearance and accent, Reese guessed him to be a New Zealander of aboriginal stock—Maori, a Kiwi.

"Did you know," he said, "that in 'stralia there ain't no railroads, north to south?"

To be honest, Reese didn't.

"With that the case, how do you suppose we do real commerce—by which I mean heavy hauling—in this part of the world? Pretty hard without railroads, wouldn't you say?"

"Never thought about it," Reese said. "So how's it done?"

"You load three or four double trailers with everything from frozen goods to toxic waste and string 'em behind an eight-hundred horsepower prime mover and drive f'teen-hundred miles due north. It's three days through the most desolate landscape on earth over dirt roads that raise dust clouds five miles long." He drained his beer, then wiped his mouth with a hand the size of a catcher's mitt. "They're called road trains, mate. And I drive 'em."

Reese said, "Let me buy you another beer."

"Nah, I got an early morning tomorrow. Headed up to the Kimberly with a haul and I'd like to visit a coupla lady friends before bedtime, know what I mean?" He took out a card and scribbled on it. "You find yourself still interested in the morning, come on by the depot in Perth. I'll give you a ride north. Name's Tuqiri. But everyone calls me Cuz."

Reese took the card. Western States Transport Services, it read, Mason Group Worldwide LTD, AU. Beneath that: Kees Tuqiri, Transportation Specialist.

"Listen," Reese said, "I'm always looking for a story. I'll be in touch."

Cuz rocked him forward with a blow to the shoulder. "You do that, mate." And he left.

The bartender was back in front of Reese. "That little bloke giving you trouble, sir?"

"Not at all," Reese said. "In fact, I think he just gave me my next project. Sounds like he has an interesting story to tell."

The bartender's friendly smile had disappeared. "Kiwis," he said, "I can't abide them. Untrustworthy dangerous lot of niggers is what they are, far as I'm concerned."

The kid shook his head in disgust and stared at the door through which the man had left. Then he turned his toothy grin back to Reese.

"Care for another, mate? This one on me."

Reese stopped at the lobby pay phones before leaving and charged a pair of calls to his MCI card. The first was to Qantas to postpone his trip back to Sydney. The second was to Denise Pierce—former girlfriend, current editor—at a glossy New York travel magazine.

"It sounds," she said, "like a good idea. Have you been drinking, Reese?"

"A little bit," he said. "Listen, if I go ahead with the story, I start reporting tomorrow. I need to know if I got an assignment here."

"We loved your piece on the Circular Quay," she said. They always loved his pieces. "You know we'll take whatever you come up with this time."

"Expenses?"

There was a brief pause. "Within reason. So tell me, what's it like there?"

He described historical Freeport with its cobblestone streets and seaside taverns. "It's nine-thirty in the evening and from where I'm standing I can smell brine on the air and there's a warm breeze coming in off the Indian Ocean."

"It's fifteen degrees and snowing here," she said. "And it's the start of the workday. I hate you. I hope you realize, Reese, what a charmed life you live."

Standing there after he hung up, looking out over the dark beach and glossy sea, he had to admit: he did lead a charmed life.

He paid the taxi-man, turned to face the activity at the Perth docks, and knew he had a story. Freighters were moored up and down the mile-long wharf—Russian, Japanese, British colors snapping in the wind, even the good old Stars and Stripes. A shadow flew overhead and Reese ducked. A seagoing cargo container, the size and shape of a train car, soared high above on the end of a boom.

Reese found the Western States Transportation Services at the south end of the wharf. The warehouse crouched along a stretch of dock, fronted by a small office with the company name stenciled on the door. A bell jangled as he walked in.

"Help you?" The clerk stood behind a counter piled with dusty files; he was black and spoke with a distinct South African accent.

"I'm looking for Kees Tuqiri. He's one of your drivers."

"Tuqiri?" the man said. He broke into a wide grin. "Hell, you're talking about Cuz. Follow me."

They passed through a door into a hangar-sized warehouse, where Cuz was studying the undercarriage of a chassis cab. The strange little man was dressed in a tank top, sagging shorts and scuffed leather high-tops with no laces.

"Got someone here to see you, Cuz."

The broad Kiwi face lit up. "This here's that adventure journo I was telling you about, Blackie. He's a Yank."

Blackie nodded, only mildly interested.

"Wait here, I'll get my checklist, show you around." Cuz hauled himself with powerful arms into the cab of the oversized truck.

Blackie said, "You're going north, with him? To write about it?"

Reese said he was.

The man laughed. "You *are* an adventure journalist."

Cuz led Reese outside. Behind the warehouse a fleet of truck trailers stood in formation.

"Man," Reese said, "I can see why it's called a road train."

Cuz grinned. "For our trip, we got a forty-five-foot tri-axle trailer, along with an LPG fuel tanker, two fridge pans, an ore tipper, and that tarped flat-top behind, for an official grand total of"—here Cuz frowned at his checklist—"just over two-hundred and twenty-thousand pounds." Cuz leaned toward Reese, smelling powerfully of sweat and last night's booze. "That's the official weight, anyway. We'll see if we can't bump it up a bit off the scales."

He was showing off for Reese, the way people did in the presence of a reporter. Cuz had more details: in addition to being nearly a quarter of a million pounds, their train would be almost as long as a football field. The prime mover was a Kenworth chassis cab, outfitted with a fully electronic Detroit Diesel and a 380-gallon fuel tank.

Cuz gazed at the silver rig as he might a woman.

"This baby's got an eighteen-speed New Venture gear box and Kittle antispin diffs, all of it riding on air suspension. In back, for our comfort, we got a high-rise aircon bunk, the whole works."

Reese duly jotted everything in his notebook as they headed back in the direction of the office.

"Only thing to worry about now is a washout. But then, that's out of our control."

"Washout?"

"Yeah, a freak monsoon in the Northern Territories. Turns the countryside into a bog for a hundred miles every direction. People get stranded up there weeks at time. But that almost never happens."

Reese said, "Almost never?"

Cuz was about to add something when a howl came from the ware-house. It was followed by men shouting and a stream of curses. Reese followed Cuz back inside at a quick trot. A group of men had gathered around a wooden crate the size of a utility shed. The man Cuz called Blackie stood cursing and holding his arm, which was covered in blood.

"Goddamn Kiwis," he shouted. "Oh, God *damn* it!"

"What's happened here?" Cuz asked.

"These stupid fuckers about cut my arm off is what."

Reese saw that the skin on Blackie's arm had been shaved as if with a wood plane. From the bottom knuckle of his small finger, along the meaty side of his hand and over the knob of his wrist bone the skin was gone, in places down to a white flash of bone. A blister the size and color of a plum was forming at the heel of his hand. Dirt and packing grease were streaked into the shredded meat, a nasty-looking wound.

"Ah, fuck, I don't feel so good." Blackie's face had gone ashy. Big jew-els of sweat had grown on his forehead.

One of the Asians led him away.

Cuz chuckled as they headed back out toward the trucks. "Blackie," he said. "Clumsy bastard's always getting hurt."

"Jesus," Reese said. "That looked pretty bad."

"What, that scrape? Nah, that ain't bad." Cuz thrust forward his large left hand. Reese noticed for the first time that the pinky and ring finger, each from just below the second knuckle, were missing. Cuz wiggled the stubs. "That's bad."

They traveled northwest along the Swan River by way of the elevated freeway. High clouds formed distant seaward towers; in foreground, from surrounding greenery, rose Perth's dazzling skyline, like some real-world Emerald City. Leaving town, the train was sent in single-trailer configura-tions, one tractor per trailer—it was impossible, Reese wrote in his notes, to drive a full road train through the city. Only after they reached the outskirts north of Perth would their real trip be underway.

Cuz, hunched troll-like over the flat steering wheel to Reese's right, recited their travel plan: northwest on the Great Western Highway to Kalgoorlie, where they were to take on cattle, then due north on the Can-ning Stock Road to Broome.

With wind in his hair, and the trailers following behind, it seemed to Reese as if they were on a joy ride.

"The ride," he said over the wind in the cab, "is surprisingly good!"

"Yeah," Cuz said with his wide grin, "but we're still on a sealed bitumen highway. Wait till we hit the dirt."

"So you're a New Zealander, right?"

"Born and bred," he shouted back over the wind.

"What part from?"

"What's that?"

"I said, 'Where in New Zealand are you from?'"

"Christchurch," came the reply.

A few moments passed by. "So what brought you to Australia?"

"Ah, this and that. Work. You know, the usual."

"In my experience people uproot for particular reasons," Reese said.

"Well," Cuz said, "I killed two men back home and figured it was a good idea to leave once they let me out of prison." His eyes gleamed as he looked at Reese. "Don't print it though, otherwise I'll have to hunt you down and kill you too. Chop you up into little pieces and throw you back there in one of them feed cars."

Reese supposed it was a joke. He turned back to watch the passing landscape as Cuz stared straight ahead.

An hour north of Perth the highway simply ended—one minute paved road, the next dirt. Cuz didn't slow as the truck hit gravel. The interior of the cab went hazy with airborne grit. A fine layer of orange dust coated everything. Behind them, the follow-trucks were lost in cloud. Reese imagined them following blindly along, elephants in a parade. Now he understood why Cuz plowed forward without braking—they were riding a 200,000-pound pileup just waiting to happen.

They deboarded at Wubin, a huddle of diesel fueling stations and cheap-eat shops. The landscape was lunar but for whorls of spinifex that clutched the earth in hardy clusters. Reese snapped photos as the men from the Perth depot worked with Cuz to couple the trailers into a road train just shy of a hundred yards in length.

It was an impressive sight. As Cuz walked around making a last minute check of the couplings and tire pressures, Reese took pictures—they always wanted pictures. His work-clothes, he noted with satisfaction, were now covered with red Outback grit.

"Good luck, mates," one of the drivers called. He climbed back into one of the smaller trucks that had followed them out of the city.

They spent the rest of the day traveling north. The sky, unhindered by cloud or tree, had a brute quality, immense and distant. Refracted light scattered into fire-ridged spectra in the cab's windshield, revealing the sun for what it was—a lonely fire raging immeasurably far above.

Cuz told a joke. "Pair of blokes goes on a road trip 'cross Oz. One sitting in the driver's, like me, other like you in the passenger's."

Here Cuz alarmed Reese by taking his hands off the oversized steering wheel. The thick Kiwi hands gripped an imaginary steering wheel above the real one, fists at three and nine o'clock.

"So they drive and drive and about six hours later driver shouts, 'Hang on, mate. Here comes a curve!'" Here, Cuz turned his hands slightly, moving the imaginary wheel to ten and four, then back again. "That," he said, "is Australia."

So it was. The road stretched dead forward, a gray plumb line, menacing in its regularity. To improve mileage Cuz left the aircon off until farther into the interior with its unbearable temperatures. The loud dusty drive discouraged conversation. As the sun sank toward the western horizon, Reese's side of the truck heated up. He slept, then was startled awake by a howl—the truck's klaxon sounding. Cuz bore down on a pick-up pulling a silver tube, a 1950's-vintage camping trailer. The rig was gaining on the little camper with alarming speed.

Cuz hauled on the chain again, a scary gleam in his eyes. "Get the fuck outta my way!" he shouted to the interior of the cab.

The Great Northern Highway, Reese noted, was little more than a narrow dirt road. The camper bounced along, shuddering, as if it meant to hold its ground. Then the driver gave way, pulled off as far as possible and sat like a dog huddling at the roadside. The train bore down, horn blaring and Cuz cursing. The pickup driver and his family cringed as the train rushed by. The camper rocked as if it were about to be sucked in under the trailers. Reese watched in fear as a great cloud of dust obscured the family behind them.

"Christ, man," Reese said. He looked at Cuz, who stared ahead.

"Fucking tourists," he said. He wore a gleeful smile, despite his tone. "They're the only true fucking menace out here. Fools don't have the bloomin' sense to know it takes a mile and half just to stop this rig."

After a moment Reese said, "It looked to me like they were trying to get out of our way."

"Nah," Cuz said. "Bleedin' tossers. You wouldn't believe what you see way out here. People on bikes, motorcycles. They'll stand right in the middle of the road, get a snapshot of you passin'."

Reese gave a nervous laugh, which he regretted immediately. He cleared his throat. "I was afraid we were going to run them off the road back there."

"Good bleedin' riddance it woulda been, too, you ask me," Cuz said. "Good bleedin' riddance."

The sun shimmered low in the sky. Still Cuz drove. He had amazing stamina, Reese had to admit. They had stopped only once to unload produce and take on a load of fresh meat to be transported northward. At that stop they'd taken leaks and had sandwiches, then headed back out. It was cooling off now—almost cold with the window open. Reese felt cooked on the side of his body facing the window. He was dust-covered, longing for a hot meal and a bed, neither of which were in their immediate future. The road ahead lead toward a whole lot of nothing.

"Aren't you tired?" he asked Cuz.

But Cuz didn't seem in a conversational mood. Reese resisted the urge to question him. They drove for some time further before coming to some sort of rest area.

Reese's body ached and getting out he felt odd, the way you felt when stepping off a motorcycle after a long, nonstop trip—as if he were walking along on someone else's legs. His joy at seeing the road house faded when he saw the place was dim inside and locked up.

"Are they closed?" he asked Cuz. He glanced at his watch, saw that it was well past one A.M.

"This ain't Sydney," Cuz answered. He was doing a walkaround, checking the trailer coupling, tires and axles, and tarps covering the flat beds. Reese followed Cuz around without much interest. There was a noticeable chill in the air and this combined with his sunburned left side, his need to eat and the general dustiness of everything was making him feel ill. His back ached—his head in an oven, feet in a bucket of ice.

The bunk compartment was separated from the main cab and accessed through a side door. First Cuz climbed in, then Reese. There was a bunk, a metal floor and a small modular step that, with the door pulled closed, served as a seat. A little TV, a satellite fax phone and a small refrigerator rounded out the appointments. Cuz used no decorations.

"Hungry?" Cuz asked.

Reese grinned. "Starving."

Cuz produced a loaf of Wonder Bread, some butter, a jar of Vegemite. Reese's smile grew strained as Cuz laid a thick layer of the stuff on flimsy bread. Vegemite was a thick and tarry spread—a yeast extract, he'd been told. It looked and tasted like something called yeast extract. It was one of the few things Australian to which Reese had not managed to adjust. But he was hungry. He accepted the sandwich Cuz offered and ate it holding his breath, chasing each mouthful with warm water from the bottle he'd brought.

"Long day," Reese said, between bites of his supper. "Do you always drive sixteen-hour days?"

Cuz chewed. Reese could see the food in his mouth. "Yeah," he said. "Sometimes more, sometimes less."

"Must get pretty lonely."

"Nah, I like the solitude." Cuz made another pair of Vegemite sandwiches. Reese declined his. "Lotta drivers work in pairs, you know. Not me. Believe it or not, there's a lot of husband and wife teams."

"Is that so?"

"Yeah. I guess you'll have to do for me." Cuz dispatched a sandwich in a couple bites. "Dainty eater like you, I guess, would be the wife."

Reese wished to brush his teeth but there was no place to do it. Cuz had clambered up in the bunk. "Coming up to bed, mate?"

Reese eyed the narrow bunk. "I think I'll just sleep here, on the floor, here."

"Suit yourself."

Reese made a pillow out of his rucksack and covered himself with his jacket. He'd slept on worse surfaces in scarier places. The bunk light went off and Reese found himself tipping steeply toward sleep.

"Hey, mate?" Cuz was wide awake.

"Yeah?"

"Mate, did anyone ever tell you where the word kangaroo comes from?"

"What?"

"Kangaroo. Anyone ever tell you where it came from?"

"Uh, no. No one ever has."

"When the Pommies came, they found all the niggers running around wild and naked, you know? Aboriginal's what niggers is called around here."

"Yeah, I know."

"When the Poms saw the 'roos, they got all rapt, as you might expect, and started asking the Aboriginals what these strange animals was. Course, the 'riginals didn't speak no English and so they didn't know what the fuck the Poms was talking about. They just kept saying 'kangaroo,' which in Aboriginal means something like, 'Mates, we don't know what the fuck you're talking about.' The stupid Poms—these men that run the world—they thought they was being told what the bleeding beasts was named!" Cuz chuckled. He had been speaking in a voice barely above a whisper, giving his ridiculous story the sound of revelation. "So now we got kangaroos."

"Interesting," Reese said. He was hoping to go back to sleep.

"You do know what a Pom is, right? What we call a Brit around here."

Reese knew. He pictured Cuz lying back in the bunk, unable to sleep and unaccustomed to company, in his shorts and tank-top from earlier. Reese propped himself on an elbow and stared into the dark while Cuz, unexpected font of Aussie lore, spoke on.

"Well, now, there's two stories about *where* that name comes from. There's those that think the name is shorthand-like, for Prisoner of the Magistrate. So many of the Brits, you know, having come over on prison ships. Get it? P-O-M."

"Got it."

"And then there's those that think it's because of the way a Brit looks, what with that sickly pinkish color of his and the white hair, the whole package looking uncanny like a pomegranate." Pommie-granite, he pronounced the word.

"Which story do you believe?" Reese asked.

There was a pause. "Well, mate, I believe them both."

"That," Reese said, "is a complicated answer."

There was an even longer pause this time. "Well, it's a complicated subject."

After this Cuz fell silent and not much later began to snore. Now Reese couldn't sleep. He was hot and cold, hungry and thirsty, he had to take a leak and the ridged metal floor beneath him felt hard and uninviting.

The diesel engine was still running, muttering away, whether to keep the cabin cooled or warmed, Reese couldn't tell. He began to worry absurdly about asphyxiating in here from carbon monoxide. He lay there for a long time—listening to the rumblings of his stomach—before finally falling into a shallow, dreamless sleep.

The bunk compartment's door stood open, diesel exhaust floating on cool air. Reese climbed from the cab. Early risers, these Outback travelers. Cuz was nowhere in sight. The roadhouse, Reese noticed, was lit up. Maybe there was a shower in there. He made his way from truck to roadhouse, the smell of grease in the air making him eager for real food. Grayness stretched in all directions.

Inside a few crusty souls slouched over mugs of tea and plates of bangers and beans. Cuz was perched on a stool at the bar. His tank-top rode up in back, shorts slung low, ass-cleavage on display for the unfortunate breakfasters. Reese took the stool beside him.

"Morning, mate. You looked so pretty lying there, I couldn't bring myself to wake you." He turned to the woman behind the counter. "Ruth, this here's the Yank I was telling you about."

Her voice was gravel mixed with cigarette ash. "A real live Yankee. What the bloody hell you doing with this criminal?"

Reese rubbed a hand over his whiskery face. "Right now," he said, "hoping to have some breakfast with him."

Reese was surprised to see that Ruth offered cappuccino. He ordered one and a plate of beans and sausages and eggs. It was served with toast and butter and a small jar of the ubiquitous Vegemite. When he finished he had another plate and a second cup of coffee. This impressed Cuz.

"Good to see you got your appetite back," he said. He looked to Ruth. "Yesterday he ate like a lady."

She considered this. "Well, he is a Yank."

A transistor radio babbled behind the counter. When the weather came on, Ruth turned the radio up and everyone in the place fell silent. Reese leaned forward to listen with them. The newest forecast was for sun and heat, but with an increasing chance of rain, possibly heavy, in the Northern Territories toward evening.

Ruth turned the radio back down. She looked at Cuz with pursed lips and raised eyebrows.

"It ain't gonna wash out," Cuz said.

"It ain't, ain't it?"

"Don't gimme that look."

"Better get moving," she said, shaking her head. She lit a cigarette. "Hope you like each other's company. And I hope you got food and water."

On the way out to the truck, Reese remained silent for a few moments, then said, "What she said about food and water. If we get stranded, do we have supplies?"

Cuz didn't look at him. He walked quickly for a small man. "Nah, don't worry yourself. In five years I ain't got stuck once. Don't intend to start today."

Reese looked skyward. The sun had just struggled over the eastern horizon and the sky seemed vast and blue and unmarked. It promised nothing but heat and glare. Maybe Cuz was one of those people with an infallible sense of these things. Well, a month starving in a mud-bog in The Kimberly with a Kiwi ex-convict would certainly make a story—maybe even a book.

Walking to their truck, Reese heard a distant rumbling and thought for a moment a storm had somehow begun to bore down on them. Cuz nudged him, looking down the road. At first there was nothing but a rising dust cloud. Then Reese realized he was watching another road train heading their way. It came on them amazingly quickly—God forbid it had to stop quickly. He watched, awed, as it thundered by, leaving a mile-high dust cloud.

Both Reese and Cuz were surprised to hear Ruth's gravelly voice in its wake.

"Looks like he's out to beat the storm."

"Ain't gonna be no storm, old lady," Cuz said, "nor a washout."

She held out a greasy paper bag. "Yeah, well, here you go, in case the two a you get bogged down," she said. "Give you an extra day to stave off thoughts of cannibalism."

They drove for several hours. Cuz's eyes took on a glaze that made Reese wonder whether the man was even conscious. Reese himself found it hard with the roar of wind and the throbbing of the giant engine beneath them to keep his chin from slouching against his chest. Some hours into the drive Cuz shouted over the noise. Reese's head came up and he was wide awake.

"What was that?" he asked.

"We passed the halfway mark. Right back there, that bridge we crossed. Can you see it?"

Reese looked in the large side mirror. He saw nothing but the blooming cloud of their wake which seemed to stretch as far as he could see.

On the forward horizon a haze was gathering. Reese couldn't tell whether it was dust or clouds. He couldn't resist bringing up the possibility of a washout.

"I'm gonna be honest with you mate," Cuz said. "While you was sleepin' I tuned in a weather report on the satellite. A monsoon's been causing coastal thunderstorms at Broome."

"What's that mean?"

"Well, warnings for heavy rains inland were being issued up and down the northwest quarter—though nothing had developed as yet."

Reese must have looked as concerned as he felt because Cuz continued.

"I'm telling you, we're gonna beat it. We pull in tomorrow, first thing if we drive through the night. Unless we get a drencher tonight, we're in the clear."

Awake now, Reese became convinced that the air had taken on a hazy humid feel.

"You're worrying, pal," Cuz said. "Why don't you have a go at it, take your mind off things."

Reese didn't understand. Then he realized that Cuz was asking whether he wanted to drive the road train. "Are you serious?" he asked.

"My thinkin' is, you're gonna write about it, you oughta drive it. Think you're up to it?"

"You are serious," Reese said.

"As a heart attack, mate."

Reese had driven race cars, piloted light aircraft and crossed the States on a Harley. He had a license back home to drive just about anything on wheels and the prospect of driving this, the longest-wheeled vehicle maybe on the planet, brightened his mood. It would look great in the article, possibly at Cuz's expense if his bosses found out he'd let a Yank drive the beast. But then, that was Cuz's problem.

They pulled over, switched sides. Reese familiarized himself with the three left-handed gear shifters and the oversized clutch-and-pedal. He had to adjust the seat back so he could fit with his long legs. Just sitting behind the wheel he could feel the awesome power of the great engine thrumming into his feet and up the shafts of his legs. He let the clutch out and throttled the motor. There was a clashing noise and the cab bucked like some huge living beast.

"Careful, fuck's sake, don't stall the fucker." Despite his girth, Cuz seemed diminutive and somehow less important seated to Reese's left on the passenger side of the cab. Still, Reese followed directions. "Remember. If you gotta stop, you just let out the clutch—and stand on the fuckin' brake and keep the rig rolling forward and for Christ's sake whatever you do, don't turn the thing."

Reese worked the truck through the first series of gears as he pulled the train back onto the road. The highway was empty as far as he could see. He took the truck up into its second set of gears and found it surprisingly easy to maneuver out onto the great dirt highway. Soon they were rolling along at a decent clip. There was wind in his hair. The vehicle seemed to vibrate as if alive.

"Cuz, I gotta ask you a favor?" he shouted over the noise of the engine and hot wind blowing in.

"Yeah, mate!"

"In my rucksack there's a camera. You mind taking a picture of me behind the wheel?"

Cuz obliged. He clicked off three or four shots of Reese working the wheel of the mighty road train.

Reese drove for a long time, impressed by the monotony of straight northbound road. The barren landscape was as unchanging as a gravel parking lot.

After a while Reese found that the world was reduced to elemental things: sky, dust, sun and truck. His mind wandered to the weather. Was that an aberrant cloud flying like a rogue flag to the west? Would they get bogged down after all?

He hardly heard when Cuz first spoke. Then there came the repeat, somewhat more urgent just beyond Reese's perception, like the sounds you hear from above water when surfacing from a dive. Then Cuz's voice reached and hauled him up from his depths.

"Mate! Look out! Wake up! Wake *up*!" Cuz's hands were on the wheel, turning it; the train suddenly threatened to tip and crash down.

The steering wheel wrenched back leftward; Reese felt his arms being pulled from their sockets. The truck was rocking violently, weaving in ever widening arcs.

"Stop the bleeding thing or we'll flip!" Cuz shouted. "For fuck's sake, man, stand on the brakes!"

Reese, panicking, stood on the brakes. They exploded with air and hissed in protest, but did not slow the vehicle.

"The brakes aren't working!" he shouted.

"Stay on them" Cuz shot back. "Give them time."

Soon the truck began slowing and came to a stop with a massive shudder that seemed to shake the entire train. He stalled the truck as it came to a stop. They sat in a cloud of dust that rose in all directions. Neither spoke for a long time. Reese's shoulders ached and his knees felt as if they were made of Jell-O.

"Mate," Cuz finally said, "I sincerely hope that that was a kangaroo."

They walked the dusty road in silence, a fine skin of dust covering their bodies. Reese's eyes stung with sweat and dusty grit. Tears welled up. About three quarters of a mile down the road he heard Cuz say, "Ah, shit."

He was standing over a crumpled gray lump. Reese was hoping he was going to find a wallaby or a kangaroo when he got there. But he knew better.

"Christ, man, didn't you see him? The idiot was right there in front of you."

"I...," Reese started but for once found himself wordless.

He stared down at the man who was dressed in grayish outback clothes. A fancy backpack he'd been carrying had been tossed some feet away. It was impossible to tell his age—his face and hair were covered in dust, giving the impression that he had been here lying on the side of the road for quite some time—not hiking a few minutes earlier, before they'd come upon him. There was not so much blood, really. The only real sign that the man might not simply be sleeping there in the road was the weird angle of one of his legs—it appeared to have been turned completely around, so that the toe was propped up on the ground beneath him. That and one partially open eye, which seemed to stare past Reese as if something interesting were taking place in the sky behind him.

"Is he alive?" Reese asked before he could stop himself.

Cuz had a disgusted look on his face. His arms were crossed as he stared down at the man. "What the hell does it look like to you?"

"There's hardly any blood, or...how could...." Again Reese ran short of words. The man's single open eye stared up.

"He bounced off the fucking bull bar." Cuz spat. He stared up at Reese, glancing against the glare of the sun. "The fuck's wrong with you, mate? Was you dreaming?"

"I was driving, I didn't see him."

"What the hell were you doin' behind the wheel, anyway?"

"You *told* me to drive."

"You told me you could!"

This was incredible, this was mad. They were standing over the body of a dead man—a man he, Paul Reese, had killed. Reese stared up one direction of the road then the other. There was nothing in sight.

Reese took out his cell phone.

"What do you think you're doing?" Cuz asked.

"I'm going to call for help. We've got to let someone know what happened."

"Like bloody hell we do," Cuz said.

"It was an accident!" Reese said. He wiped at his face and licked his lips. Again he looked up and down the road. He repeated his words in a quieter tone: "It was an accident."

Cuz took a step toward Reese, leveled a finger at him. "You put that phone away, or there's gonna be two bodies laying out here in the road."

"Cuz, man, look. We can explain ourselves. They'll see it was an accident. Anyone can see that. How much trouble can we get in?"

To Reese's shock, Cuz snatched the phone from his hand. "If they find out I was letting an idiot Yank drive the car, I'm in as much trouble as you. We're not telling no one *nothin'*, you got that?"

Cuz began marching fast back toward the truck. Reese stared down at the poor dead man. He felt a surge of panic. What had he done?

He ran to catch up with Cuz. "Listen, we can't leave this man in the middle of the road here. We hurt him."

"*We?*" Cuz said. He kept moving toward the truck without a glance at Reese.

"Look, I didn't see the guy, okay? I just.... I don't know how but I didn't see him. But no matter what, we can't just leave him there."

Cuz arrived at the cab and hauled his thick little body up. A strange wind, heavy with humidity and the smell of wet, was blowing. The sky was going green, a Kansas-storm look to it. Cuz grabbed a bag and a tarp and hopped back down.

"You're right about one thing," he said. "We can't leave him there." He still wore the same disgusted look. "If it was an Aboriginal, maybe we could. But this fucker is white."

Cuz scanned the road both ways, then removed a collapsible spade from a sleeve. The man dug, ignoring Reese's protests. He worked furiously until he'd opened a hole about three feet deep in the orange earth. He stood up, lathered in sweat, mumbling under his breath. He walked past Reese to retrieve the tarp.

Cuz lined the hole with the blue tarp. A piece of the cloth extended just beyond the rim of each side of the shallow grave.

Grave. The word dazed Reese. He watched as Cuz walked to where the body lay. Cuz looked down at him for a moment, hands on his hips, with a strange expression, something hovering between pity and fascination. The man of course had not moved. Cuz shook his head—was he expressing sadness or mere disgust? A large drop of sweat, then another, dropped from his forehead and landed on the man's cheek. It left a clear stain, like a grotesque tear, beneath his partially open eye.

"This is insane, man." Reese was numb. "This is crazy. We can't bury this man."

Cuz said, "Just two minutes ago you said we couldn't just leave him. Now you don't wanna bury him. Make up your goddamn mind."

Cuz pulled another tarp from the duffel and spread it near the man's body. Then he got down on one knee and rolled the man's body so that it flopped hideously and lay face down, half on, half off the tarp. His foot now pointed skyward. There was a sickening gash on the back of the man's skull that made his head looked like a flattened melon. Hair was matted around it.

Cuz was resting on one knee, his arm crossed over the other. "Are you gonna help me here, or do I have to do everything?"

Reese staggered a few steps away and threw up. Then he fell on his knees and found himself sobbing into the dusty earth. He wished he was home. He wished he couldn't hear the grunts of Cuz at work behind him. When he finally turned, he saw that Cuz had dragged the tarp to the hole and rolled the man into the grave. Cuz walked past Reese again without a word, grabbed the man's backpack, and threw it in on him. Then he re-filled the hole with earth. He left Reese there staring at the shallow grave of the man he had killed.

Reese walked back to the truck. A cool wind was blowing in from the northwest. He was shivering. Through his shock he heard a savage clanging noise. When he walked around to the front of the truck he saw Cuz swinging the stubby spade baseball-bat style against the tubular metal of the bull bar. Cuz swung it with huge powerful arcs. Reese wondered how he could do it, metal on metal, without hurting his own arms. The bull bar clanged like a bell, tolling with each blow. Each time he struck the bull bar a dent appeared, deforming the metal. Cuz went on striking the bull bar until he seemed exhausted. He dropped the spade back in the duffel.

He looked at Reese. "Don't want," he said between breaths, "someone to look at the bull bar and see the shape of the bloke's head you hit and all his blood."

Rain clouds gathered as they drove. A bank of them were flying up, stacking; he could feel the charge on the air coming through the window. They drove through the Great North Desert and entered The Kimberly from the south. Reese saw none of it. In his head he kept replaying the rumble of the truck, the look of the dead man's single open eye looking up past him. What had he been doing out there hiking? Where had he been staying? Would his family have missed him by now? What was his name?

Sheets of heat lightning shivered on the far horizon. These were soon replaced by forking tongues of lightning, the color of blue steel and bone. The first fat drops of rain spattered against the flat windshield; the sun disappeared behind ugly thunderheads. The stone-dry, cracked-earth riverbeds began to run with water, ropy rivulets that writhed and grew and seemed alive.

For a long time neither spoke. They drove into the darkening night, and through it. Water pounded down, a biblical rain. The lightning continued, back-dropped by a spectral night-palette of crimson, violet and jaundiced yellow.

Sometime into the night Reese realized that the spinifex and tough acacia trees of the desert had given way to greenery, suggestive of lushness and a foul tropical ripeness. When he closed his eyes, Reese saw the dead man in the desert looking up past him toward the sky; it was better to keep them open and watch the surreal light show and listen to the thrumming rain.

Cuz said, "This rain looks bad, but it ain't. We beat the worst of it. We ain't gettin' flooded in."

Reese nodded. He stared ahead seeing nothing but flashing lights, the curtains of rain and strange shadows that seemed to dance at the side of the road.

Cuz said, "It wasn't really your fault, mate. That idiot was in the middle of the road. The bastard got what he deserved."

They drove for many miles before either spoke. This time it was Reese who broke the silence. "It was an accident," he said.

Cuz's expression remained inscrutable in the glow from the instrument panel.

Reese woke from unsettling dreams that he couldn't remember. Amazingly he had slept; amazingly Cuz was still driving. Rain drummed the top of the cab.

For a moment Reese felt a surge of joy that they had gotten through the deluge the night before—that they weren't bogged down like some vast black swamp. Then he thought of the young man's eye staring up the brute sun the day before.

"Look, up ahead," Cuz said.

Buildings dotted the roadside and Reese saw date palms and fields of grass. Lightning lit everything briefly, and then the world went gray.

"You awake?" Cuz asked.

Reese waited for a few moments. Then he nodded. "How about you?"

By way of answer, Cuz drove on.

Reese waited by the truck in the rain as the trailers were decoupled at a depot outside of Broome. For the first time in years he smoked a cigarette. It made him feel dizzy and sick to his stomach. The rain came down in sheets. He could taste it, it seemed to get into his nose, the flavor of drowning in fresh water. He smoked another cigarette.

They had uncoupled the last trailer and Cuz was recording something on his clipboard when a small green and tan car pulled up. There were overheads rigged on top, a provincial Western Australia police car. A lanky cop unfolded himself from the car, stretched and then put on a Smokey Bear hat wrapped with plastic. He adjusted his rain slicker and looked around. Reese watched with a mixture of relief and dread as the man came their way.

"G'day, mates," he said.

"G'day," Cuz responded. Reese had the feeling that he was observing some strange Outback ritual beyond his understanding. The cop gave Cuz a look that was hard to read. He touched the brim of his hat for Reese.

"Pulling in from Perth, are you?"

"That's right," Cuz said.

"Pretty nasty weather," said the cop. "Your trip north okay?"

"It was dreamy," Cuz said.

The cop turned his blue eyes to Reese and back again. "Suppose you came up by way of Kalgoorlie Road and the Northern Highway."

"Only route I know of," Cuz said.

The cop nodded and smiled. He walked around to the front of the truck and then came back again. He looked at Cuz, then Reese for a long time.

"Is there something we can help you with, officer?" Cuz asked.

"No, mates. It's just that we got call of a body being washed up on the road back a ways a bit. Looked like a kid'd been hit. By something big."

"That so?" Cuz said. He glanced up from his clipboard and then back again as if he were talking about a melon that had dropped off the truck.

"That's right," the cop said. "You wouldn't know anything about that, would you, now?"

Cuz frowned and shook his head. He scratched his neck. He was wearing the same clothes he'd set out in two and a half days before.

"Who's this?" The cop meant Reese.

"This is an American journalist came along for the trip. He's writing about road trains."

"Oh, yeah," the cop said. "So what'd you think of the trip?"

Reese exhaled smoke. "It was very interesting."

"A journalist, eh? Writing a book?"

Reese coughed into his fist. "No, just an article."

The cop gave him another long unnerving look. "Lemme guess. Don't know anything about the dead man, either?"

Reese struggled to hold himself still. Beside him Cuz was studying the clipboard.

"No," Reese said. "I don't know a thing about it. Sorry."

The cop squinted at the dull sky. "Looks like the Wet's arriving a little early this year. Fitzroy River's over its banks. It's impassable to the south already. You're not heading this thing back south any time soon, I reckon."

Cuz said, "I reckon not."

The cop nodded. He looked at Reese again, then smiled. "You write about me, write something good, mate. And pick a nice-looking bloke to play me in the movie."

"I'll make sure," Reese said.

The cop got in his car and drove away.

The cab smelled of the sweat and dust of the last two days. "You done good, mate. That was the right thing to say."

Reese made no answer.

A sign welcomed them into Broome. Cuz said, "Never did ask you who you're writin' this for."

"*Condé Nast*," Reese said.

"I ain't never heard of that newspaper," Cuz said.

Reese laughed, first softly, then harder. Beside him, Cuz didn't utter a word.

They drove into Broome, a wild-west grid of streets and leaning tropical trees. The wind and rain had died down somewhat, which, according to Cuz, meant the real rain was about to come in. Reese wasn't listening. He watched from the rig as they drove through Chinatown and into Hamersly Street, past the Post Office. Cuz parked the truck in the lot in front of the Kimberly Klub and watched as Reese climbed down from the truck.

"Remember. Keep your counsel," Cuz said.

He winked and the gesture seemed to seal a collusion from which there was no escape. Having lied, Reese was bound to a future course of lies—each denial bringing more attention to the previous ones, making them harder and harder to explain, if he ever should have to.

The rig erupted with black smoke and shuddered as it left Reese behind. A yellow truck stamped BROOME PIANO MOVING followed in its wake.

Reese checked into his room then left his bag with the bellman. He went to the bar where the bartender offered his hand.

"Pleased to meetcha."

"Charmed," Reese said.

He sat with his drink and kept his own counsel.

The dead man's eye looking past him came into his mind. He pushed the thought away. Thinking was a problem. He ordered another drink, and then a third and settled on a plan. He would go to his room, drink some more, a lot more, and turn on his computer. He would write—writing was always a good substitute for thinking. It would be a thinly veiled account of what had happened, maybe fiction even, who knew? He would call it Road Train, publish it, collect his check, move on.

Javier's Silence

I found myself gazing at the altar of the dead in the *Central de Autobuses* in *Calle Colón*. A typical display: candied skulls placed among photos of the dearly departed with hand-scrawled messages to the other world. On a bed of flowers before the skulls rested a row of colorful toy coffins. Paper skeletons with demented grins and wide sombreros capered overhead at the ends of invisible lengths of wire.

A clutch of costumed children raced by calling for candy and coins.

"*¡—saliendo con destino al Distrito Federal!*" The last call for my bus echoed through the corridor. I picked up my bag and walked with the crowd toward the door.

The vast station, overcrowded even at this hour, occupied several city blocks. A fat October moon squatted above the city. I worked up a sweat lugging my bag along the curb where lines of people waited to board the overnight buses.

I passed the *autobuses de primera clase*, road liners with smoked windows and plush reclining seats. Next came the *clase de economia*. Me? I was headed for the last row, the *camiones colectivos*—soot-stained jalopies that muttered like senile old men at the dusty end of the lot.

A small mob waited beside the last bus south. The driver flashed an unpleasant smile and offered to take my bag. But I had lost too much luggage and paid too many bribes to be so easily tricked. The man reeked of beer and cheap *pulque*. I climbed onto the bus and found a seat near the back and sat alone.

In the aisle a woman approached and glanced at the open space beside me. She was one of those graceful creatures you saw rarely in Mexico. Tall, fair-haired, misplaced on a midnight bus, a swan in a horde of bats. I smiled but she averted her eyes and took the last empty seat, which happened to be in front of me.

Behind her came a fat norteño with a bristly mustache and soiled clothing. He, of course, sat next to me. I observed from the corner of my eye as he jostled my bag trying to shove his own under the seat in front of us. He sat back and glanced my way self-consciously. "Good evening," he said in Spanish. "My name is Javier."

I turned to the window before he could continue.

With a gnashing of gears and a great belch of diesel fumes our trip began. The bus lurched along the rutted lot and out onto the paved surface of Lopez Mateo. Javier's generous ass occupied much of our seat and his meaty shoulder bounced against me no matter how far toward the window I crammed myself.

There was also the matter of the man's smell. My own humble budget and my body have taught me tolerance in this regard. But Javier had an odd and deeply unpleasant odor that I couldn't readily identify, something worse than sweat that forced me to breathe through my mouth.

Javier stirred his bulk and jostled me as he leaned forward. He made wet breathing noises. The head of the woman in front of us turned, then turned back.

"*Pinche,*" Javier huffed, reaching for his bag. His paw-like hand flailed. I leaned forward and snatched his bag from under the seat and handed it to him.

"*Órale,*" he said. "*Grácias, amigo.*"

"*No hay de que,*" I said.

"Ah, American," he said in Spanish. "*Gringo.*"

"Everyone has to be from somewhere." Light from outside slashed his face as we drove.

"I espeak English, is no so much." When I didn't respond he became embarrassed and reverted to Spanish. "*Hijo guey*, you have perfect Spanish. Where does a *gringo* learn to speak so well?"

I wondered why natives felt the need comment about my Spanish if it was so good. But I knew the routine. I nodded and thanked him. I told him I had worked for a very large American company many, many years before and after quitting had stayed in Mexico. I raised the international signal for him to leave me alone. I opened a book to read in the shadowy light from the window.

Javier searched his bag. He removed a newspaper, a pack of cigarettes and a little transistor radio. He fumbled a cigarette out of his pack, lit up and blew a large cloud of smoke.

I couldn't help seeing the headline of his newspaper. *¡LA INVESTIGA-CION CONTINUA!* it screamed. There were colorful crime scene photos in the Latin American manner. The heat, the bumpy ride—not to mention Javier's unpleasant odor and now cigarette smoke—were creating *un dolor matador*, as the Mexicans put it, right behind my eyes.

"*Oye, cabrón*, have you heard about this?" He tapped the paper with his cigarette. Ash fell like dead rain onto his belly. "This *madness* going on?"

"Another one?" I spoke reluctantly. But, of course, I was curious about what the paper had to say.

"Yes, another one. Less than a week ago. Do you live in a cave, my friend?"

So now we were friends. "Another couple."

"Exactly," he said. "*Este es un cabrón, hombre.*"

It was an strange thing to say about a killer and the way Javier said it hinted at admiration. Since spring the town had been in a state of delicious panic because of the murders. The victims were all young couples, well-off, found in cars parked around the fashionable *zona rosa*—the bodies were left in strange poses surrounded by candles in cryptic arrangements, an occult message no one understood. The FBI had supposedly sent men to help the local police. It was all very exciting, something out of a Hollywood thriller. When some insignificant fool from the Monterrey police mentioned Jack the Ripper, the press pounced; and the Zona Rosa Ripper was born. *Reeper*, the Mexicans pronounced it.

Javier appeared to be something of an expert on the whole affair. "Three couples," he said. "Now four, just since winter, *cabrón*. Look at these pictures." He held the paper in my face but I didn't need to look.

"This *cabrón*, what a monster! You see here, how the police believe that he keeps souvenirs from the killings? The heads are removed—" he made a plucking motion with his thick fingers "—and always the head of the woman is nowhere to be found." He licked his lips. "What do you think about this, *amigo*? You're an American."

As if any American was an authority on such matters as drug smuggling and serial murder. I told him things like this happened everywhere, sometimes even outside of the United States.

"You're right about that, man. The police have theories about this *hijo de puta*. Personally, I think maybe he knew these people."

"*Knew* them?" This I asked against my own better judgment.

"It is all very intimate, you know, the way they were killed, the places they were found." He turned his bulk more my way. "The police believe him to be a drifter. But in my mind, I think this could be something different. I read books on the subject."

I told him I did not care. That it was a matter for the police. He smiled as if maybe he'd expected better from me.

"Imagine," he said loudly. "Perhaps this *cabrón* has a collection of the heads of women in his home somewhere? A shrine to murder. One can only wonder what else the Reeper takes."

The lovely specimen in front of us turned with an angry expression on her face, but Javier was too intent on his theories to notice. She caught my eye and shook her head, a gesture of sympathy, before turning back to her *novela*.

Javier went on but I stopped listening. I didn't want to encourage him by commenting on it, but a week earlier I had stood across the street from a *zona rosa* parking lot after new victims had been discovered, surprised to find myself in the crowd, as police investigated by the lurid lights of their patrol cars. The entire city had been swept up in a dark and strangely thrilling fever; and with it came a heightened sense of community that no one cared to admit. Of course the flip side of this was mutual mistrust, suspicion and fear.

We passed through the *barrio antiguo* and the forlorn trainyards of the industrial south, then entered the scrubland of the Nuevo Leon desert. The landscape was barren but for the occasional agave farm, the plants themselves scattered, alien, rising like inverted daggers from the sterile earth. A shocking number of dead dogs littered the roadside.

I must have slept. I awoke to find that we had parked beneath the lamp of some nameless station. Javier was gone but his bag was still beneath the seat. I considered leaving my own, but already we were taking on new passengers, the driver was nowhere to be seen, and I didn't want to take any chances. I shouldered it and headed to the building.

A Day of the Dead shrine had been erected near the door, where small votive candles gave off strips of smoke in the heat. People had gathered at a greasy counter where greasy *antojitos* were for sale. I passed the counter and found the *cajera*—she was more interested in the TV flickering in the corner than in me.

"*Disculpe, señorita. ¿Donde quedan los baños?*"

She glanced at me then back to the TV. "*Aqui no hay baños.*"

"*¿Como que no hay baños?*"

"*Pues no hay, chavo,*" she said. She had a tuft of coarse hair at the corners of her mouth like an Asian man. "*Tendrás que utilizar la casita afuera.*"

The key was attached to a filthy length of twine. I was offended more by her use of the familiar voice than by the fact that I had to use a Mexican outhouse. The bus driver saw the key dangling from my fist and made a show of tapping his wristwatch as I passed.

Behind the building the dusty yard extended into darkness. It was hot and desolate back here and utterly silent. I smelled the *casita* before I ever saw it.

Stepping from the outhouse I found that my eyes had adjusted to the dark. I was standing in a graveyard of discarded bus and truck parts. Weeds bristled up between the slats of an old radiator grill and a tree had somehow managed to grow through the exposed gear teeth of a differential assembly, an arthritic claw clutching skyward. The rusty skeleton of an ancient *camión* sagged in crepuscular light.

I heard growling and turned my head. A pair of black dogs reeled from the darkness, snapping viciously at each other's throats. From the junkyard a third dog charged toward me. I froze in place, mesmerized by the sight of its bared fangs. How utterly absurd, I thought, to be attacked by a mad dog in a dusty Mexican junkyard!

Suddenly a heavy stone flew from behind me and struck the animal's snout. The beast yelped and fell headlong into the gravel. It shrieked in a human voice as the other dogs tore into it with flashing teeth.

A few feet away the bus driver waited, another jagged stone in his hand. He leered with alcoholic eyes. "You should be more careful," he said. "In this place, even the dogs are evil."

I was aware of Javier's freakish odor as he let me pass to my seat. He seemed agitated in the unnatural light from outside.

"Have you heard, *guey*? Did you hear the news?"

"What news?"

"*¡Cabrón!* The killer, he struck again! It's all over the news." He raised his transistor radio for me to see. "They found two more bodies this very evening—another couple, *cabrón*! This is incredible—horrible!" He said this the way an heir to a fortune might describe news of his horrid old grandmother's death.

The bus groaned and lurched into motion. Random light made crosshatches on our faces as we pulled back out onto the highway.

Javier had the radio against his ear and was listening intently. He shook his head occasionally; he chuckled a couple of times. It was hot and I was beginning to wish I had eaten something back at the station.

Javier lowered the radio from his ear.

"*Cabrón*," he said. "This *pendejo* is...I don't know what. The police believe these murders to have been committed *last night*. He took the head of the woman again—or so the news says."

He leaned toward me, an intimate gesture.

"I once read a book, which I believe was made into a movie, and in this book a very rich young American, a—" and here Javier flipped into English "—how do you say, a guppy?"

I had to think for a moment. "A yuppie?"

"Yes, yes. A jopey. A guppy is something else, no?"

"Yes."

"Well, in the book this jopey is an important man by day, rich, but a killer by night. He is of course a user of drugs—" as if all Americans were "—who stalks young women and lures them with his money and good looks back to his townhouse in Manhattan Nueva York, I think it is."

"It would be."

"And in this book, the man removes the head of one of his beautiful female victims and what does with do with it?" Here he leaned in even closer to me. "He puts it upon his, you know, his *penis*." He repeated the word for my benefit in English. "You understand? He places it upon his upright member and frolics around his apartment lit only by candlelight. He does this to see himself at play in the many mirrors he has positioned about. Do you believe perhaps our killer is inspired by this book and is doing the same with his victims?"

The swan in front of us had turned once again, shocked and disgusted. She looked at me now with disapproval, as if it were somehow my fault.

Javier saw, and shrunk back, finally embarrassed. He tried to recover. "It is interesting, no, the coincidence?"

"Javier," I said, "I would rather not talk about this."

He nodded, ashamed. He had an unpleasant, bloated face and I noticed that his bushy mustache was there to cover an ugly scar, a pink, star-shaped welt running from lip to nose. Presently, he closed his eyes and leaned back, I hoped, to sleep.

We climbed into the bleak hills of the Sierra Madre Oriental and the air grew dry and cool. I have always enjoyed the singular stillness that possesses a train car or plane cabin late on an overnight trip and I stared through the window peacefully. Javier bounced against me and soon he began to snore. He would do so lustily for a while, before gasping on his own wet breaths, which would cause him to thrash and mumble. Then the cycle would begin again. But even this failed to bother me, hypnotized as I was by the steady procession of nothingness outside my window. My head rested itself against the cool glass and I drifted off.

Some time later I felt a poke in the side. I blinked, surprised to have found myself dreaming. The bus, I realized, had stopped.

Javier's round face hovered beside me. I yawned and stretched and tasted my own sour breath.

"Are we picking up more passengers?" I asked.

Javier's head wagged back and forth. He seemed frightened. "No, *cabrón*. The *guardia* have stopped us. No doubt, they're stopping all the buses going south."

Outside stood several men in the flashing lights of a roadblock. This is a part of the world where the *policia* are more dangerous than the *banditos*, and Javier's concern was understandable. A pair of cops boarded, characters from a comedy: one short and fat, the other tall and cadaverous. Supposedly they were searching for the Reaper. But these men had no intention of catching a killer. It was just an obvious pretext for robbing us. I was irritated by this bad luck and could barely hide my contempt as they worked their way down the aisle. It was maddening, sitting there waiting patiently to be stolen from.

The tall *guardia* stopped at our seat.

"*Gordo*," he said, "What's in your bag?"

"*Nada, señor*," Javier said.

The man's gaunt face reminded me of the skulls from the station in Monterrey. "If it's empty, then open it and let us have a look."

Javier handed his bag to the cop, who searched it, made a snorting noise. He threw it back at Javier. "You've got money?"

"Not much," Javier said.

"Come on," the *guardia* said. He counted out the bills Javier produced. "This is all, fat man? Are you really so poor?"

"It's all I have."

The cops eyes fell on me. "And you, what are you doing here?"

"Taking a trip to Mexico City," I said in Spanish.

"A *gringo*. Going to Mexico City. Well, well." He looked at my bag. "And what do you have in there? Marijuana? Guns for rebels?"

"Clothing," I said.

"Open it."

I said, "No."

"Pardon me?"

"I said no. You have no reason nor right to look through my things."

The cop's left eye twitched almost imperceptibly. A cruel smile coiled beneath his mustache. "You know, of course, that I could arrest you, beat you and leave you to rot in jail?"

"And how would you explain the fact that all I have is clothing in my bag? How would you explain that you have stolen money from these decent people and still have found no killer? Perhaps the newspapers and the *gringo* FBI would be interested in learning how you conduct this manhunt of yours."

His tongue flicked out to taste his mustache. Then he made a dismissive gesture and laughed good-naturedly. His bony hand fell on my shoulder.

"I like you, *gringo*. You have balls. How much money do you have?"

"None," I said.

"Ah, but now you go too far."

I always kept a few pesos on hand for muggings and for bribes. The cop snatched the bills from my hand.

"You're lucky," he said. He smiled as his grip tightened painfully on my shoulder. "We're so busy on this investigation that I don't have time to split your face open." He released my shoulder and ruffled Javier's hair. "Keep your boyfriend here in line, fatso. He'll get himself into trouble."

Javier had remained silent in the presence of the *guardia*. Now that they were gone, he released a new flood of chatter. "*Puta*, your Spanish is perfect like a Mexican."

But my head ached and I had grown sick of Javier's voice.

"*Pinche, cabrón*, you're crazy. I've never seen a *gringo* with such *cojones*. What *do* you have in the bag? It's drugs isn't it? Only a *narcotraficante* has such balls."

I stared at Javier. Still he continued.

"That cop. He was afraid of us. You could see it in his face."

I said, "Javier? Look at me. Look in my eyes."

He looked.

"I'm going ask you a favor." I said this quietly and in Spanish. The headache roared behind my eyes. "Shut the fuck up. Do you understand me? I want you to place the two deformed halves of your ugly mouth together and breathe through your nose. I want to hear no more noise from your fat, disfigured face."

Javier blinked once, and sat back. My headache blinded me, as if I were looking through a pair of my old grandmother's reading glasses, as if I were a child all over again.

"Please," I said. "Please just shut up."

I felt grungy and feverish, my head still hurt and my body had brewed a ripe gravy in its various folds and crevices. The air warmed as we descended from the hills. In a few hours the sun would rise and some time later we would arrive in the *Distrito Federal*. But now I wanted a shower and a bed and to be free from this endless bus ride.

Beside me Javier seemed to have forgotten my cruel comments from earlier. Inane chatter floated over on his vile breath. I made no response.

We arrived at a PeMex station outside of San Luis Potosí. We deboarded and shuffled like living dead to the station. Javier accompanied me, hustling to keep up. He patted me on the back.

"*Cabrón*, you can leave the bag in the bus. It's safe there." He winked. "Even if it is filled with drugs."

"Nothing," I said, "is safe in a place like this. No one is in charge."

Rolled tacos and soggy *syncronizadas* were for sale at a steam table near the cash register. Javier followed me to the counter. He watched in amazement as I consumed taco after taco. They were greasy and flavorless except for the fiery chiles I piled on them.

"*Hombre*, slow down," he said, "you'll explode."

I finished my tacos and half of his. Immediately I felt a hot churning in my gut. I looked around desperately. My stomach rumbled like something under a volcano. I stood in a panic. A sign pointed the way around the side of the building to the *sanitario*.

It was a disgusting hole that reeked of urine and worse. Filthy rags choked the sink and mosquitoes hovered near my face. Behind the door of the stall I found a foul toilet clogged with shit and piss. Used toilet paper littered the floor. I hesitated, then dropped my bag and slid onto the damp seat.

As Javier predicted, I exploded. There was heat and grease and then burning liquid. After this came unspeakable cramps and icy sweat. I emptied myself, racked with shudders. Missing the bus was the furthest thing from my mind as my distress went on and on.

I was clammy and weak but the cramps had passed. I looked around only to discover that there was no clean toilet paper—only the used paper on the floor. I remembered the filthy rags in the sink. I stood and made my miserable way from the stall to the disgusting sink.

Javier awaited me when I emerged. We were on the building's far side and though it was a public place, we were very much alone. I remembered my cruel remarks earlier. Perhaps Javier had reconciliation on his mind, perhaps murder. The moon had flown behind some clouds and the back lot was utterly vacant.

"*Cabrón*," he said. The scar had twisted his lip into a sneer. He pushed his jaw toward my bag, which was over my shoulder, and made a step toward me.

"You carry it everywhere, don't you, *gringo*? Even to be sick. I wonder what it is you carry that needs such protection."

A breeze tousled Javier's hair. He was a strange man—knock-kneed, fat. A pathetic example of humanity. I say this as a man who is himself rather oddly proportioned—with quite long legs, a short but powerful torso and a grotesquely large head.

I said, "Would you like to see, Javier? What I have in the bag? Would you then be quiet?"

He nodded eagerly. I beckoned him closer. I unzipped the bag and held it forward for his inspection.

A smile played around his mangled upper lip. "*Cabrón*," he said. His eyes met mine. His expression grew round and pale. "*¡Dios mio!*"

I felt much better—headache gone, gut calm. I took my seat as the driver made his final call. We left the station behind. We had driven for some time before the delicious thing in front of me turned to regard the empty spot where Javier had been seated.

"Your 'friend,'" she said. "He deboarded in San Luis Potosí?"

"Yes. I believe it was his final destination."

Her eyes rolled upward—whether to indicate the roof of the bus or the vacant heavens above I could not say.

"I thought," she said, "that I noticed a pleasant silence."

I smiled in agreement. "You're traveling to Mexico City?"

"To Cuernavaca," she said, "to meet my fiancé."

"Ah," I said. The word rolled off my tongue: "Cuernavaca."

Her smile was like a thousand moons. "Your Spanish is really quite nice."

The first rays of daylight bled over the eastern horizon. Beneath the seat in front of me I slid Javier's bag in the space where mine had been. I placed a small votive candle, then another, on the empty seat beside me, mindful of Javier's deep and merciful silence.

The Pleasure Thing

The papers arrived that morning by post. Keller sat reading them on the way downtown from his apartment in Klongtoey. When he finished, he placed the papers in his briefcase. Then he stared out at the filthy water of the Chao Phrayah River so intently that his driver didn't utter a word. They sat like that, in silent battle with the traffic, all the way to the office. So now it was official: David Keller was a divorced man.

His boss, Hedgewick, greeted the news as he did everything, with jolly good cheer.

"Finally," he said over Keller's desk. "And about high fucking time too, if you don't mind my saying so."

"Actually," Keller said, "I do."

"Celebrate," Hedgewick said. "What you need is to get out of this place early and do fuck all. No worries, I'll take care of you."

Beyond Keller's office window the river snaked southward, teeming with small boats and ferries. Canal piers grew like teeth along both banks. The Hotel Sofitel—postmodern, pagan—rose from a clamor of buildings on the far shore.

At three o'clock Hedgewick was back in Keller's doorway. "I'm knackered. The fuck you Yanks say, anyway? It's Miller time."

Keller gestured at the paperwork on his desk. "Too much work."

"I'm the boss. If I say we're done for the day, we're done. Let's bugger outta here."

Hedgewick chatted with the limo driver in Thai. After months of classes, Keller could count to eight and ask for tea. He had no aptitude for a language that to him sounded like alley cats fucking. Monks in saffron tunics waited for them to pass through an intersection. On the corner an ancient woman was burning a pile of votive money; thick braids of smoke coiled into the hot sky.

"Mate, you're thinking way too much." Hedgewick's hand came down on Keller's shoulder. "You need a little nip."

The console between them served as a combo armrest and wet bar. Hedgewick opened it, pulled out a decanter of Scotch and poured them each a measure. Keller drank while Hedgewick took another call.

When he hung up, Keller said, "You know, Robin, I'm starting to have new respect for Vietnam veterans."

"Oh, fuck's sake, you're not in that mind-set I hope."

Keller smiled. It occurred to him that Hedgewick had already been drinking. "I'm serious. Look out there."

Hedgewick looked.

"I mean, this place is crazy. I know how much you like it, but it's crazy."

"Yes," he said, "crazy. But most pleasurable. "

"They pay us thousands of dollars, they treat us like kings. And still I find it uncomfortable. They dropped those guys in rice paddies out here and tried to kill them."

"Christ, you're morbid. That was *years* ago. Give this man another drink, he's too morbid!" Hedgewick poured more Scotch. "You know what your problem is, Keller? You're bored. Bleeding Yanks. You're in fucking paradise and yet you somehow contrive to be bored."

"I'm not bored. I'm just not good at the pleasure thing, not like you are anyway."

Hedgewick laughed once, a yelp. "'The pleasure thing.' Bleeding Americans. You're all zealots, you know. Moralists and fanatics. Dangerous thing abroad, a bored Yank who thinks too much." Hedgewick's phone sounded. He winked and stage-whispered over the shrill voice on the other end: "Trust me. I'll cheer you up."

They stopped at several fancy bars, Hedgewick haunts, where the man charged round after round to the company expense account. After the fourth or fifth place, Keller was floating along in an amber mist of Scotch. He had waited calmly beside Hedgewick at the curb in front of the Hotel Oriental for what seemed like a long time, before saying, "Hey. What happened to the car?"

"Cut it loose, mate, sent the driver home. It's just you and me, now. More fun that way."

Hedgewick led him to the choked avenue where cars crept along at walking pace. A metered taxi pulled up but Hedgewick waved it on. "We'll never get anywhere in one of those devils, not at this hour of the day."

Keller noticed, to his surprise, that the afternoon was fading fast. Soon it would be evening.

He turned to comment on this to Hedgewick, who was busy waving his arms. A *tuk-tuk* clattered up with a noise like a lawn mower gone mad.

"You're kidding," Keller said.

Hedgewick gave him another of his winks. "When in Rome...."

The *tuk-tuk* was a motorized rickshaw, a deathtrap on three wheels, named for the noise it made. The driver gripped motorcycle handlebars; passengers rode on an open bench behind.

Hedgewick was making steering motions with his hands. The driver spoke no English, but could tell Hedgewick wanted to drive. He shook his head, smacked himself, made his own driving motion—"No, *I* driver."

Then Hedgewick came back in fluent Thai—a favorite trick he played with locals. The driver was so surprised by *farang*'s mastery of Thai that he relented.

The tiny man climbed in back and tried some Thai on Keller. "Not me," Keller said. "I passenger."

Hedgewick rocketed the *tuk-tuk* into traffic, and the driver realized too late the terrible mistake he'd made.

"Nooo!" he howled as they careened from one side of the street to the other. Hedgewick weaved through traffic, whooping. He plunged toward the back of a parked truck, wheeled around it at the last possible moment, scaring a group of pedestrians into the middle of the road.

They turned onto Sukhumvit Avenue—wide, crowded, chaotic. Hedgewick flew down the center, raced past cars and trucks in front of them, dodged others in oncoming lanes. Horns blared, people cursed. Above it all rose Hedgewick's laughter and the driver's beseeching cries.

At Soi 33, entering the diplomatic sector, Hedgewick turned too sharply. The *tuk-tuk* went up on two wheels, nearly tipped, then righted itself. They plunged onward. Keller closed his eyes. He sat very still.

Hedgewick parked on a side street and climbed off the driver's seat. He towered over the driver, laughing. The driver jabbered shrilly until Hedgewick handed over a thick wad of bills.

Lights were coming on now and the night vendors were setting up their carts. In the narrow alley, a boy was fitting an ornamental halter on an elephant. Its eyes—large, brown, long-lashed—revealed deep sorrow, as if the animal grasped its plight and was ashamed: a majestic beast, imprisoned to do tricks for pennies from tourists. The image triggered a fit of dark laughter in Keller. It surged up from some shadowy place, uncontrolled, nearly hysterical.

Beside him Hedgewick broke into a wide grin. "What, eh?" he asked. "The fuck's so funny?"

Keller's vision blurred with tears. He had stopped to bend over as ugly laughter came over him in a spasm.

Hedgewick slapped his back, laughing now himself. "See. I told you we'd be having a good time before long."

At the end of the alley stood the Full Monty, faux English pub, a Hedgewick favorite. It was a dark, wainscoted space with remaindered cricket gear on the walls. They were greeted at the door by the Thai manager, a girl they both knew, dressed in sneakers, khaki culottes and a golf shirt. She clasped her hands and bowed her head.

"Good evening Kuhn Robin, you enjoy self tonight?"

The girl called herself Apple, a nickname to replace her unpronounceable Thai name. Apple was a pet of Hedgewick's. He walked with his arm around her toward a table and let her practice her English on him.

"Yes, Apple," he said. "We enjoy self tonight."

"Kuhn David, too?"

"Yes, Kuhn David enjoy self, too. He enjoy self every night now—he divorced. Isn't that right, Kuhn David?"

Keller smiled without enthusiasm.

"So we *all* enjoy self?" Apple said.

"Sometime we do."

The girl smiled. "You make fun me, Kuhn Robin?"

"Me not make fun you," Hedgewick said. "Me *like* you."

"Me like you, too, Kuhn Robin."

By the time she got them to their table a little waitress was setting out a pair of mugs.

"*Gawd*, this place is good!" Hedgewick said and let his hand slide to Apple's bottom. She turned quickly, bowed with a smile, backed away.

They dispatched the beer with alarming speed and ordered another pair. In the manner of pubs everywhere, the Full Monty had suddenly gone from mostly empty to totally packed—the typical after-work expat crowd. Men and women in suits, westerners all, laughing, drinking too much, enjoying themselves thoroughly. How could they? Keller wondered. How could they?

Hedgewick disappeared to take another call. On the TV a cricket match was showing on Star Sports. Keller had to squeeze one eye shut to see it. There was a break to a Star Network programming ad—they were showing a baseball game later that night, broadcast live from the States. A perfect, shocking picture of home came to Keller. He was there, part of it, standing on his green suburban lawn with his wife. Suddenly his scalp crawled and he went hot all over. Where was he? What was he doing in this place? How had he come to be a clerk in a distant, lonely hellhole? What had he done with his life? He found it suddenly difficult to breathe.

Hedgewick saved him with a slap on the back and a slur of beery words in his face. "Wake up, Keller, we've some friends here. Look lively, pal."

Keller followed him to a table crowded with a group Hedgewick ran with. Hedgewick plopped himself next to a woman who worked at an investment bank in town. Keller was pretty sure Hedgewick was banging her on the side. Her husband, who worked for UNESCO or something artsy like that, was sitting right there beside them, all of it out in the open, the way it was with these people. Fucking expats. There were a few other faces Keller recognized vaguely but didn't know. More drinks were brought.

Keller became aware that Hedgewick was trying to signal. Keller heard his own name spoken. He turned. There beside him was a woman with hair pulled back in an after-work ponytail, dressed in a charcoal suit. He gathered, through the din, that she was the one saying his name.

"Keller? David Keller, right? Don't you remember me?"

"Yes, of course, of course, I do," he said. He was desperately trying to think of who she was. "Please, have a seat—*Cindy*."

Bingo on the name. She slid onto the chair beside him as drunken memory raced to his aid. Cindy Something-or-other was American, from Indiana or somewhere like that. Hedgewick had introduced her last year at a cocktail party. Cindy had just been finishing a divorce, Keller trying to avoid one. Good old Hedgewick, always there to help. Keller had met Cindy exactly once, for lunch. She seemed lonely then, but Keller's heart hadn't been in it then.

It was now. She pulled a strand of hair behind her ear, smiled, lifting her shoulders up. It was the sort of little-girl gesture that Keller didn't usually go for. But tonight it seemed charming.

"It's *pouring* out there," she said.

People shouted to be heard over the music. A thick slab of smoke clung to the ceiling. Through a window Keller saw rain—torrential, early-evening, Bangkokian rain.

"Don't tell me," he said, "it must be six o'clock."

She laughed at the joke. "It's a bloody ty*phoon* out there."

She was, he remembered, one of those Americans who picked up and used all the obvious Brit phrasings she heard. But what the hell, no one was perfect—he sure wasn't.

"You know," he said, "I was just thinking about you a few days ago."

"No way," she lied back. "Because I was just thinking about *you*."

They bantered about nothing for a few more minutes. How beautiful, those flat Midwestern vowels! Keller ordered her a drink and a beer for himself. He caught Hedgewick leering from across the table with moist lips.

The subject turned to news from home. Keller mentioned the baseball game he'd seen announced on the Star Network.

"Baseball," she said through smoke. "I'd give *any*thing to see a baseball game."

"To have a hotdog with mustard on it and drink a beer?"

"Oh, my God, it sounds better than sex. Well, *almost* better."

Keller's mood lifted. He thought about inviting her to his apartment to watch the game later. But that might be too forward, even among expats. Instead, he told her about the papers that had arrived that morning. He showed her his bare left ring finger. It looked somehow significant there under the bar light. He asked how she was getting along following her divorce. She said it was just fine.

"You get used to it," she said. "You'll see." She peered at him through cigarette smoke and made the girlish gesture again. "Good-looking men don't stay lonely long over here."

He smiled. "Listen, I don't think that waitress is ever coming back. I'm gonna go get our drinks."

"You're sure?"

"Sure I'm sure," he said. "Believe me, it's my pleasure."

He waited at the busy bar. When he caught Apple's eye, she hurried over to take his order—knowing Hedgewick, after all, did have certain benefits.

"It's turning into a beautiful night, Apple," he said. He drummed a light beat on the bartop.

She nodded. "It rain, but soon stop."

"Rain is good," he said.

She passed him the drinks with another smile. "Kuhn David now enjoy self, fo' real," she said.

"Fo' real," he said. "Kuhn David *hope* enjoy self."

He tipped her extravagantly. He weaved his way through the crowd as best he could, sloshing booze on himself.

Back at the table his seat occupied by another man—a journalist he'd met around, a guy called Cummings, who always dressed as if he were about to leave on safari. Keller set the drinks down in confusion. Cindy turned to Cummings. "Do you remember David Keller. He's *American*."

"Sure," Cummings said. He shook Keller's hand. He had no idea who Keller was.

Hedgewick had disappeared again and now there was no place for Keller to sit. Cindy made a show of looking around for a chair. For a minute it looked bad, but an Australian came to Keller's aid—the man shoved over, gestured at the seat. Keller sat. He sipped his beer. Cindy was smoking a new cigarette and saying something he couldn't hear.

He leaned forward with a strained smile. "I'm sorry?"

"Thanks," she said. She made a drinking motion with her cigarette hand, an ugly gesture. She laughed. "For the drink." Keller sat back as Cummings moved his hand over Cindy's thigh.

Women. Keller pretended to be engrossed in the TV. The Aussie beside him tapped his shoulder.

"You're a friend of that buggerer Hedgewick, aren't you?" he said.

Keller admitted he was.

"He's a fucking drunk, that one." This seemed to strike the Australian as funny. He laughed and said something to his friend, who ignored him. He was pretty drunk himself. "Listen. I'm supposed to tell you the fucking queen's on the phone."

"The Queen?"

"Hedgewick, you nit. He's a fucking queen, you know, a mad bugger, that one. He's on the phone."

Keller thanked him.

"No worries, mate. You're American?"

Keller nodded. The man was tall and slender with hair cropped so short you could see pink scalp beneath.

"This fucker here, he's not speaking to me now." He jerked his thumb toward the man beside him, whom Keller figured to be his boyfriend. "People can be a fucking prick."

"They can," Keller agreed.

"Been to Australia?"

Keller had. "Perth," he said, "Melbourne, Sydney."

"Sydney's a right hole, isn't it? A rotten hellhole, that place is. It's where this tosser's from."

No Hedgewick in sight. "Well," Keller agreed, "there is something about Sydney, an essential Asianness about it, that gets on your nerves."

"What?" the Aussie sneered. "Did you hear that? 'Essential *Asianness.*' Gimme a fuckin' break."

Keller stared at the man. Then he found himself standing.

Cindy said, "You're not leaving are you?"

"No, no," he said. "Bathroom."

Cummings gave him a kindly look.

Making his way through the crowd, he could hear the drunken Aussie behind him: "Asianness! Did you hear that? What a lot of stupid rot. Fucking *Asianness!*"

The rain had passed. A wet city smell came up from the pavement. The night markets were open now, the streets more crowded than ever. Vendors flourished spits of roasted meat over shooting flames.

Keller wandered out onto the main avenue. An unsettling cacophony poured from the doors of bars and restaurants: Khmer rock-and-roll, American top forty. Thai women in spangled dresses teetered on heels, dangling like jewelry from the arms of Russian mobsters who looked silly and murderous in disco suits.

He turned into a side street. At the end of the alley the Thai boy was pulling a chain, trying to get the elephant from earlier to move. Behind, another boy struck its legs savagely with a bamboo pole.

A group of men squatted around a large metal tub filled with beer cans. They fell silent as Keller blundered into the alley. The harsh angular faces flowed in the sinister light of a dream. He stumbled and went down to one knee. There was laughter. He righted himself and found himself walking quickly, then running. The laughter went on, a phantom chasing him down the alleyway.

He was surprised to emerge back on Sukhumvit Road. A hand clapped his shoulder.

"Bloody hell, Keller." Hedgewick's face loomed large and florid. "Here you are. I spend all day lining a good time up for us and then you disappear."

"I think I'm getting a taxi home," Keller slurred.

"I'm not leaving you alone on a night like this, pal." Keller was flooded with boozy affection for Hedgewick. "Not a chance, mate. You're coming with me."

They loaded into a taxi. Hedgewick gave the destination: Patpong.

The go-go clubs were going full swing. It must be late, but who knew? Keller seemed to have misplaced his watch. They walked down the street, Hedgewick beaming at the girls who called from sidewalks. Patpong was a hideous, seductive place. Keller had been here only once before and then had hurried through, the way he might pass a rack of pornographic magazines back home.

"I don't know about this, Robin," he said. "Maybe we should just go home."

"Nah, no worries, pal. This is your special night. Just relax, and have a good time. Ah, here we go."

Keller followed Hedgewick to a bar entrance. They were greeted by a violent-looking man in a Fu Manchu beard and draped in several gold chains. He took money from them. The bar was dark and smoky.

"Scotch," Hedgewick told the bartender, "a pair, on the rocks, one for me and for my friend-in-need here."

Keller wrapped his fist around sweating glass. Women lounged everywhere, some in tight, whorish dresses, others in schoolgirl skirts and fishnet stockings. Here, there was something for everyone.

"You know this place?" Keller asked.

"I know it," Hedgewick said, "but it don't know me." He drained his Scotch. "Stay put. There's someone I have to see."

Keller sat at the bar, self-conscious, out-of-place. He sipped his drink. Suddenly the room lurched and seemed to go spinning around him. He closed his eyes, which made things worse. When he opened his eyes, Hedgewick was there with the scary-looking man from the front door.

"On your feet, pal."

They followed the man down a smoky corridor where shadows crept on the walls. At the end of the corridor they entered a room furnished with a pair of sagging sofas.

The doorman gestured for them to sit, then disappeared behind hanging beads.

"Wow," Keller said. "Okay. Wow." He tried to smile; his fist was opening and closing. He made it stop. "Robin, I'm not so sure about this."

Hedgewick ignored him.

The beads rattled. The doorman walked in behind two young girls in blue jeans and halter tops. Neither could have been more than fourteen years old.

"Oh fuck," Keller said.

Hedgewick grinned, showing eyeteeth.

"These two for you." The man addressed Hedgewick. "Both ver-juhn."

"Yeah, right, whatever." Hedgewick forked over some bills. The man said something to the girls. One came forward and sat on the sofa close to Hedgewick. When he began speaking to her in Thai, her eyes lit up. The other sat on the edge of the couch beside Keller.

She was a beautiful child, mocha-skinned, slender as a sylph, more like something of air or sea than of land. Her face was smudged with makeup, inexpertly, which somehow made her even more sickeningly attractive.

By sitting quite still, Keller managed to keep her at bay. Hedgewick's girl had curled up on his lap. She was speaking to him in low tones, rubbing the inside of his leg. The sight was revolting, exciting. The man from the door observed with little interest.

Keller's girl glanced at the doorman, then turned her large eyes to Keller. "No like?" she said. She pouted. "No want me?"

She slid closer to him. He felt a jolt when she touched his arm with her small hand.

"I like," he said. "It's just not good."

Hedgewick's girl had gotten up and was standing to one side.

"Ah, mate," Hedgewick was saying to the doorman. "They're both lovely creatures. Lovely. But we'll take that one." He pointed at the girl with Keller. He said something in Thai. The man led the first little girl away. Hedgewick watched her go, wistfully, then stood.

"Where you going?" Keller asked.

Hedgewick was adjusting his trousers. "I lined this up for you, mate. It's your special night, not mine. One can't do this sort of thing every night of the week."

"No," Keller said. "Wait."

But Hedgewick laughed, backing through the beaded doorway. He bowed deeply in the Thai manner. "Enjoy self, Kuhn David. Try and get the hang of that pleasure thing."

Keller wanted to leave. Yet he stayed. The little girl had kicked away her sandals. She had perfect tiny womanly feet. She stood and placed her small hand on his wrist.

He followed her to a windowless room lit by a bare bulb. A narrow bed, a sink with a rusty basin. On a side table stood a tiny, carved elephant and a large, glass bowl filled like a candy jar with wrapped condoms.

She moved her body against his. "Want make love?" she asked in her child's voice.

He took her by her narrow shoulders and held her away from him. "No," he said, "please, this isn't good."

She pouted. Her eyes were distant. "Not good, not want make love?"

"No, *this*—it's not good, you see, it's bad. He was aroused, God help him. "This is a bad life for you."

"It not bad," she said, "it good. It real good, Big Guy." She stood on her toes and kissed his throat and he recalled the first time he'd had sex with his wife. They'd been kids, both in college. She was a sorority girl, a virgin, or so she'd claimed. He worked on her for weeks and when she finally gave in, man, she couldn't get enough: in cars, bathrooms, cheap hotel rooms—his young ex-wife-to-be fucking him like a whore before they were ever married. Had it been a straight line from that to this? Where was he? What was wrong with these people and this place? With him? With everything?

"No," he said, "it's bad, this is bad. This isn't good for you, it's a bad life. It's all bad."

"No," she said, "it *good*."

She tugged him toward the bed, then pressed against him.

"Come on," he said, "don't."

"You like?"

He shook his head. Her small hand touched his belt, then slowly slid down.

"No!" he shouted. He meant only to push her away, to put some space between them. But his hand swung up and struck her chin. Then he punched her twice more, hard, with his fists. "I said *no!*"

His fist was drawn back to strike again and he stopped.

The little girl had reeled onto the bed. Her head lolled like a bulb on the end of snapped stem; her eyes swam.

"Oh, my God," Keller said, "Oh, Jesus, I'm sorry. Oh, fuck, I'm so sorry."

He stepped toward her, but she cringed in fear. Blood came from the corner of her mouth.

"No," she said, "I sorry!" Her jaw didn't seem to be working right. "I sorry, Mister!"

"Oh shit," Keller said. "Oh Christ. I'm so sorry."

"I sorry," she mimicked, cringing back. "It bad life."

"Oh God." Again he tried to approach but she kicked frantically into the corner of the bed.

"*I* sorry," she said. "It bad!" She said it hopefully, pathetically. "It *bad* life!"

"Shh," Keller said, as he might soothe a crying child back home. He raised his hands, then held them to his head. "Oh God."

The little girl's voice was beginning to rise now, threatening to become a wail. "It *bad* life!" she cried. "Bad!"

"Shh," Keller hissed, "*please.*" He wiped his mouth, then dug into his pockets. He took out all the money he had and threw the notes on the bed beside her.

She was howling now. He hesitated for another moment, then fled through the doorway. Beneath the music from the bar he could just barely hear the girl, shrieking now, a hysterical noise.

He raced through the bar. Hedgewick was gone, of that he was sure. The doorman gave Keller a curious look as he passed. Outside he smelled the river and saw scores of people swarming in the garishly lit street.

Now he was scared. Would he be followed from the bar? He imagined he could still hear the girl's cries behind him. A ragged piece of newspaper scuttled along the dirty sidewalk.

A hand fell on his shoulder, turned him around. Behind him stood a thin man in a linen suit, a westerner.

"Oh, sorry," came the drunken voice. "Thought you were someone else."

Keller pulled free and moved into the dark street. Look at the people, he thought, all of them searching for something, though he had no idea what. He mixed with the people, swam with them—the businessmen and sailors, the local thugs and the thousand other strange creatures of the Bangkok night—hoping simply, finally, to disappear.

Macho

Kate Broadstreet was hated by al-most everyone in her employ and that was fine with her. She was blunt and demanding, one tough broad, she liked to say, second-in-command at Mason International de Mexico, S.A. It was an important job. People talked: she was being groomed for something big, she had *rockets* in her shoes. Even her boss, a powerful old-timer ready to retire back to the States, trod carefully in her presence. Her successful campaign to land a controversial, but massively lucrative, telecommunications contract with the Mexican government had raised her profile even higher within the company. When it was announced that both the CEO and the President of Mason Group Worldwide—a pair of men who famously despised each other, who used underlings as disposable pawns in a global game of one-upmanship—were planning to attend signing ceremonies in person, she naturally took charge of the event.

"Goddamnit," she said at a meeting of senior staff. This was Monday; the brass were scheduled to arrive the following Saturday. "I'm tired of hearing you people piss and moan about this visit. It's an opportunity for every one of us at this table, and *I* intend to take full advantage of it. If any man in the room isn't up to the job, he can get the hell out of here right now, no questions asked."

Eyes were cast downward. The old man, her boss, observed the performance in silence. She was the only woman in the room.

"Good," she said. She cast her gaze across the wide mahogany table. "Next, I want a new keynote presentation"—papers exploded like flushed birds from her hand—"this one sucks, I'm not presenting this crap. And I want a full accounting of why we're over budget on the press event. If someone's playing hide the sausage with costs and I find out, I'll hide his sausage for him. Who's in charge of VIPs and the press?"

One timid hand rose.

"Okay," she said. "Any further questions?"

As usual, no one uttered a sound.

She stalked the executive suite after lunch to make sure her will was being done. She was forever amazed at the trivial junk people kept in their offices: artwork of product on the walls, job sites—okay, that made sense. But cartoons, family pictures, pictures of pets even? It was a miracle that any work ever got done in this place. One of the few battles she'd lost with her boss was a campaign to rid the office of these petty distractions, these signs of weakness. Her own office was a model of sparse utility and she felt everyone else's should be too. But the old man, a creature from a different era, had for once overruled her.

Coming around a corner she overheard her name being spoken. She slowed to eavesdrop on a pair of account executives, Pierce and Sanchez by their voices.

"... and said she wanted it rewritten. *All* of it."

"Then I would rewrite it."

"Oh, I will. But what a bitch."

"This is true."

"A regal bitch."

"Shh. The walls, they have ears."

She strode into plain view. The two of them, these so-called men, fell into silence. She stared them down but didn't say a word—let them sweat, wondering whether she'd overheard. She approved, of course, of their sentiments.

At five P.M. the old man's head poked into her office. He was of ancient vintage, a relic from the days when men ran the world over gloomy lunchtime martinis in midtown Manhattan. He took a seat.

"Kate, I don't want any problems when Bob and Bob are down here."

"You think I do?"

He toyed with one gold-plated MGW cufflink—more meaningless decoration. "Weren't you just a little hard on the boys today?"

"Those jerks? If I had a whip I'd take it to them."

He grinned. He liked her foul mouth and took advantage of the opportunity to play good cop with the staff, a shrewd old buzzard. "They're scared to death about this deal. Truth be told, even I'm a little nervous. But not you."

"Why worry? We'll blow the Bobs away. They'll make a ton of money. They'll love us." By which she meant, *me.*

He smiled, trying to figure her out. "I'll buy you a drink. We'll talk about the Bobs behind their backs."

"Too much work," she said. She was the only person in the world who ever turned him down for a drink.

She left the office at seven p.m. Frightened minions stared at computer screens as she passed. In front of the José Cuervo building, she hailed a green and white taxicab. Twenty-five minutes later it dropped her at the sidewalk before a disreputable *taverna* near the *Zócalo* in the red light district. Dark men sat hunched over glasses, following her with probing eyes as she crossed toward the ladies' room, this important woman, an attractive *gringa* in navy suit and expensive creamy turtleneck sweater.

She closed the stall door behind her. First, she removed her expensive shoes and fine stockings; the gritty tile hummed with electricity on her bare feet. She slid free of her slacks and panties and then came blouse and bra. Her nipples stiffened in the damp air. She shook her hair from its tight bun. From her bag she removed open toe pumps and a tiny red shift dress. She stepped into the dress and slithered it over her hips, the hem rising to mid-thigh. The material was like a whisper on her bare flesh. Using a cracked mirror above the tiled sink basin, she dusted her cheeks with rouge and painted her lips the color of dry blood.

The air was hot and tropical on her bare thighs when she left the bathroom. The same dark men now gaped as she crossed the planked floor. In the sky, dangerous clouds converged with the threat of rain; she knew they would pass, unspent, to the mountains in the east. Lights were coming on throughout the garish block. A car stopped. The young man at the wheel had exquisite black hair—like something carved from wood—pale lips and sharp cheekbones, the face of a Toltec warrior. The eyes were concealed behind dark glasses. He ordered her to get in the car.

She got in.

"You changed clothing, as I told you to, in the *excusado*?"

"Yes," she breathed.

"No underwear?"

"No, Bernardo."

"Did I tell you to say my name? Don't look at me. Look down."

She obeyed immediately, fixing her eyes on her exposed red toenails.

He drove in silence. They passed through the shadowy Bosque de Chapultepec. The car paused for traffic where Avenidas Insurgentes and Reforma formed crossroads, and she gazed upward at the virile statue of Cuauhtémoc, with his broad shoulders and plumed crown. On a nameless side street they stopped before a building with crumbling stucco walls. He led her upstairs to a room lit by a single dim bulb.

"Go," he said. He pushed her toward a small bed.

The smell of must and sex filled her head as she fell on threadbare sheets. He pulled the pumps from her feet and straddled her. With lengths of coarse rope he called *soga*, he tied first her hands, then her feet to the metal bed posts. He blindfolded her.

"You want me, don't you?" This he whispered in her ear.

"Yes," she said.

"Yes, what?"

"Yes—*señor.*"

"Ah," he said. "The men in your country, how like women they must be."

"So true, *señor.*"

"Like little boys with no idea how to properly please a woman. They're afraid."

"Yes. And weak."

"A *gringo*, an important one, who I recently drove to the *correa de toros*—the fighting of the bulls—he grew pale and weak at the sight of the bull's blood and the death throes of an old mare. Is this a man?"

Excitement had trapped her voice in her throat.

"A true man fears nothing. This is the essence of *machismo.*"

"Please," she said, "touch me."

Abruptly Bernardo stood. "Now I will make you wait."

A match sizzled with the odor of sulfur and smoke. He didn't speak. She imagined him standing above her with contempt. Desire spread through her, something viscous, dark and strange.

"*Please, señor,*" she said.

"No."

After a long time he crossed the room away from her. A window scraped open. Street traffic could be heard, a child crying and there was the smell of ozone and imminent rain.

"Please," she begged. "*Now.*"

But tonight he refused her his touch, not so much as a kiss to the throat or a stroke of his fingertips on her hot thigh.

Some time later he freed her from the rope. He removed the blindfold from her flushed face. Restless clouds bucked in the dark sky. They drove through the strange Mexican night in silence. She walked through the massive doors of her home alone—trembling, desperate, mad, insane with desire.

"*Goddamnit,*" she growled the next morning.

She surveyed bowed heads at the wide conference table in her office. "What the hell's the problem with you guys? Didn't anyone bother to check the tie line? Didn't it *occur* to anyone? It's only the president *and* the CEO of the fucking company we're keeping on hold."

She glared, furious, at the speakerphone in the middle of the table. Each time the secretary keyed in the code, the phone returned a steady mindless beeping.

"The circuits," the secretary said, "all are busy."

"Then let's all unbusy them. It's a tie line. It's supposed to *tie* directly to the States!"

Finally the call went through. A peon 2,000 miles north picked up and told them to wait. They waited. Some time later the voice of Bob One—the president—boomed over.

"Broadstreet? Kate? That you there?"

"It's me here, Bob. We got the whole executive floor of MGW de Mexico sitting here trembling and waiting for you. Say hi, boys."

The boys, embarrassed, said hi.

Bob barked the old man's name, had to, but his real business was with Kathleen Broadstreet. She debriefed him on the deal—six months of bare-knuckle, balls-out negotiation with corrupt officials, endless struggles with a hostile press, merciful silence from the indifferent citizenry. She did not fail to remind her audience of the sums involved—enough money to make a pharaoh blush. Talk turned to lighter topics: the public event, a gala, speeches, a factory tour, where the helicopter would pick the bosses up and drop them off.

"Presidente Wolfe sends his regrets but he will be unavailable to attend," she said.

"Shocking," Bob said.

"The V.P., of course, will show for the grip and grin."

"Biggest deal this year, and *both* of us coming down for the gig. You folks must be scared shitless down there." Bob gave a cruel little laugh.

"I myself stayed up late trembling last night."

"Kate!" Bob Two had come on the line from Dubai. "Is it gonna rain? It sure as hell better not rain, I wanna go hunting over there with the old man."

"If it rains, Bob, it's because I want it to. If it rains, it's because we *arranged* for rain with good reason."

Both Bobs howled with laughter. About the only thing they agreed on was their mutual esteem for Kathleen Broadstreet.

The Bobs' voices melded into one. "What time are you picking us up at our hotels, Kate?"

Since the finest hotels in Santa Fe had only *one* presidential suite, the bastards had to be booked into separate hotels, budgetary restraint be damned.

"I'm not picking anybody up. You guys pay me too much to drive a shuttle. My personal driver will arrange your ground travel. I'm leaving his pager number with the concierge."

"That's our gal!"

The call ended. Men shuffled from the office.

"Good job, Kate," the old man said. He was too close to retirement to care that she had outshined him. "The Bobs sure do love you."

"Yeah, well, there's still the event to worry about."

The old man's eyebrows went up. "Is that a note of anxiety in your voice?"

She told the secretary to call her driver upstairs. The old man was leaving as the driver entered.

"I want to make sure you're available this Saturday morning. Make sure to line up a pair of other drivers for the big bosses." She was sorting through papers on her desk as she spoke.

"Yes, madam, of course."

"Keep your schedule open. I expect this to be a very stressful weekend. Very stressful."

"Yes."

He turned to leave.

"Oh, and Bernardo?"

The slender young man turned his sharp features back to her and finally she looked up. He pierced her with a raptor's gaze.

"Tonight," she said in a quiet voice, "I have to leave late. I'll page you."

"Of course."

He left her in San José in the noisy square where pickpockets and fire-eaters plied their trades. Men prowled a row of porno theaters. Tonight, he told her, she would walk the street like a whore until he picked her up. She felt a thrill throughout her body as she moved with the crowd in the tawdry streets. She walked for a long time before turning right at Calle Hidalgo with its food stands and beggars. In the distance rose the Monumento de la Revolución and the lights of the Gran Meliá. Tonight a cool breeze brought the threat of rain but once again none came. Eyes devoured her short skirt and bare legs with animal greed.

Bernardo had been assigned as her driver two months before and it had been lust at first sight. She knew almost nothing about him except that he had trained as a young man to fight bulls, and had washed out of that strange sport at an early age. Like many failures, he could talk of nothing but his broken dreams, and he viewed all of life through the violent prism of the bullring. But he owned a square jaw, a rock-hard ass, and an abiding cruelty that appealed to her. Their peculiar affair had gone on for six weeks: in that time he had tied her and cajoled her and stroked her and licked her to the quivering edge of climax but no further, teasing her like prey. It drove her mad. It also made her fierce and clear-minded at work, like a boxer who starves himself of sex to hone a killer's instinct. In his presence her knees felt liquid. Was he watching her now from a distance? Was he somewhere in a bar drinking, leaving her alone among these hungry people?

She turned onto the main avenue and found herself before *La Fuente de Diana la Cazadora*, the fierce goddess wild-haired, flourishing her bronze sword. Kate became aware of eyes on her. In the shadow of the statue stood a small man, staring at her with eyes set narrow in an over-large head. She moved along in her high heels. A few blocks further on she spotted him again; he'd followed her, leering with dark lust, his eyes dead and full of secrets. Kate was a woman who instinctively attacked what frightened her and she returned this man's stare through the crowd, displaying the most vicious expression she could conjure. He blinked once, then scurried into shadows like a rat. When she crossed the spot where he had lurked, something cold remained, the sensation of swimming through a cool current in a warm stream.

A hand grasped her waist and she drew a sharp breath. Bernardo tightened his grip and led her down an alley.

"A man," he said, "has control in all situations and fears nothing. This is the first principle of *machismo*."

Her mind hummed with street noise and the rush of blood in her ears. Above, lightning rippled through the tormented sky.

"Pain is something to be enjoyed."

"Yes," she whispered.

"One who understands this can control anything—even that most difficult thing: oneself."

Bernardo forced her against a wall. The brick was cool and damp as if the building were suffering a cold sweat. "Tell me," she said, "about true men."

"A man invites danger. He takes desperate chances. What else is being in the ring with a bull? Risk. A fight to death, always—the beast's or one's own."

He had pulled the skirt over her hips. She closed her eyes and pressed her face to the cool wall. Her nails clawed the sweating brick.

"To be *macho* means that one shall always speak truth. One must say precisely what one believes in all situations."

"Please, *señor*," she said, trembling. "Tonight."

Calloused fingertips crept along the length of her inner thighs.

"A man is a creature who denies himself all pleasures and accepts pain. A man understands that pain *is* pleasure."

"Please."

Another ripple of lightning, a breeze.

"*Please.*"

In her ear with hot breath he hissed, "No."

One day before the Bobs were scheduled to arrive, the office was running a fever. Kate called men to her suite, dispatched high-paid executives on petty errands across the city, demanded run-throughs of presentations only to cut them off two minutes in. She snapped up men who came unprepared into her office and spat them out. She was on fire, untiring.

Harris stopped by to ask whether she needed to hear his presentation. His devious confidence energized her. She told him to get out of the office, go get a drink, go home and rest. He seemed surprised. He turned to go, but she called him back.

She looked at him for a long time before speaking. "You make or break your career tomorrow," she said. "You realize that?"

He paused. "Yeah," he said. "I guess I do."

"You *guess*?"

He shrugged. "It is what it is, Kate."

"Okay," she said. She winked. "Good luck."

At five, the old man was in her office, offering to take the boys for drinks and some R&R before the big event tomorrow. Did she want to come along?

"There's more to do when I leave," she said. "I intend to be fully prepared when those two show up."

The old man watched from the wall window at the end of the executive floor as she crossed the street. Mike Harris appeared beside him, arms crossed, looking down.

"There goes one tough broad," the old man said. "I don't know how she does it."

Harris watched as she climbed into her chauffeured car and headed away. "I wouldn't mind knowing her secret myself."

A breeze entered through the bedside window. The room was dark and smelled of shadowy autumn. Tomorrow would be her shining moment, her opportunity to seize the ring, to go to the top of her field—to *win*. But now she lay face down, blindfolded, hands and feet bound. Surrender made her powerful. To understand weakness made her strong.

Bernardo spoke. "Tell me where I am."

"You've just opened the window," she said, after a moment. "I can feel the breeze on the backs of my legs."

"Good," he said. "I am standing on the chair. I have removed my shirt."

"Yes."

"I am beautiful," he said.

She pictured him shirtless, lithe, possessed of predatory grace. He was beautiful. "Yes," she said.

"I am *macho*," he said.

"Yes," she said. "And am I? Am I *macho*, Bernardo?"

"You are!" he said.

She heard him step from the chair and approach the bed where she lay. His breath was urgent on her neck. "Do you hear outside, what's happening?"

"No."

"Listen."

She strained to hear what he wanted her to hear. She heard wind, an angry growl of thunder and—"*Rain*," she whispered. She felt it now, the slightest mist spat in by the breeze.

"So, then," Bernardo said. His hands worked miracles. She shuddered. She moaned. "How very much alike they are," he said, "the sounds of love and of death."

He moved closer, closer. She gasped.

"They say that in the end, after having been taunted and exhausted, the bull *invites* the matador's sword." He shifted his weight; he paused. "It is of course widely known that at that moment they become—one."

"Oh," she said, "*señor!*"

The Dangerous Season

We were minor league drivers then, racing cars in Caracas. This was in the years between the most recent coup and previous dictatorship, one of those short-lived times of South American stability during which even normal people could cobble together lives while waiting for the next political or economic or climactic catastrophe. Our team was an informal community of four, expats among expats, young men a long way from home, in a strange country, living on the fumes of racecar dreams.

Fulo Carbijal, the crazy Cubano from Miami, was on our team that season, and so was the Brazilian boy-wonder, Luciano Negri, just nineteen, a kid with such a pretty face that we renamed him DiCaprio. Next came my good friend Rod McCourt, a Scotsman, a speaker of perfect Spanish, the one everyone said was going to make it big. And then there was me, the Old Man, twenty-nine that spring, a permanent exile, four years in Venezuela. I'd run through a lot of luck and promise, and I dispensed free advice, the wisdom of the years, to anyone willing to listen.

I called a meeting for the first of May, a sticky morning full of rank, green smells and diesel exhaust. It always reminded you of where you were: in South America—in fucking *Caracas*, man—hungover, an important race just a few days off.

Fulo was first to arrive at the grungy café near my apartment on Parque Central. He shuffled up in a bright, tropical shirt and shades over his eyes. "Old Man," he said. He took a seat. "My stomach and head, they're killing me." *Keeling me.*

"They're punishing you for what you did to them last night," I said.

This was the end of the rainy season when rivers swell in the mountains and bring down tropical water that makes everyone, even the locals, sick. Fulo touched his temples with great tenderness. "This is not the tequila sick-rise, man, this is the evil water. It turns the bowels so that you can't walk upright like a man."

How many times had I said it? *Don't drink the water.* He nodded, his expression grim, a cramped look we knew well. Dysentery, like lack of funds, being a condition we frequently shared.

DiCaprio arrived with hair slicked back and a Brazilian-English dictionary tucked under his arm. His only ambitions were to drive Formula One cars and learn the King's English. As yet, he had achieved neither. "Fulo, mate," he said. "You appearing to be messy, rather. As well as to be dying."

Fulo wiped away a mustache of sweat. "Easy for you to say."

The café door opened one more time. Street noise and the stink of burning rubber rode in on a wave of hot air.

Rod closed the door behind him. Gym-built muscles bulged under a polo shirt. He was all Scottish and bluff, filled with offensive good cheer. "Morning, mates," he said. He took a seat and asked for coffee.

"Fulo is to appear not well," DiCaprio said. "Is the water."

Rod shook his head. "Not listening to the Old Man, *Fulito*?"

"The bad water, yes," Fulo said. And now from beneath his dark shades, a grin. "Of course, I'm also terribly hung over."

"Rather do detect the stench of a distillery about this table."

"Stench?" DiCaprio said. He flipped through his dictionary. "Distill-ery?"

Breakfast came. Thick, black coffee, hard rolls. Rod spread pages of the *Racing News* among the plates and we began to talk. Who was on what team? Who was in, who was out? A group of cocky young men, overconfident, gossiping, a sewing circle. I pointed out a story about a French driver we knew. He'd crashed his Formula One car in Australia the week before. His legs were ruined, almost lost one of them. Worse, he did lose his sponsorship. This Frenchman had driven with us in South America before breaking into the big leagues. He was bad news, a dirty driver, the type to pull ungentlemanly stunts that put the whole field at risk. You didn't exactly laugh at this sort of bad luck. But one was surprised to see it come to this.

"Lost his ride," DiCaprio said in disbelief. "Of the big time."

I shook my head. "He always was a dirty player."

"He was an *hijo de puta*, man," Fulo said.

Rod said, "You get what you deserve."

There was the hush that always followed talk of bad luck. We finished breakfast without a word and I was sorry that I had brought the French-man up.

It was Rod who finally broke the bad luck silence. He slapped his hand down on the back page of the *Racing News*. He said, "Here it is, boys, just the thing to kick off a new season."

He held up an ad for a bar. I couldn't read the name but I saw the bad east-side address. It didn't matter, Rod said. The place had good-looking girls, cheap drinks, a racecar theme—what else did you want? "Let's go tonight," he said.

"Yes," Fulo said. "We can be heroes there."

"It is for those other of you too bad," DiCaprio said, "that I'm so much better looking than you and perhaps more talented as driver."

"Another bar?" I groaned. "Tonight?"

Rod said, "He can't keep up with the youngsters."

We paid the bill and walked out. The sun hammered down. In the green park across the avenue punks in bright-colored T-shirts sold stolen wares. An old drunk with a skeleton's face watched us from a park bench made of stone.

"My head!" Fulo said, "is *killing* me!"

Rod got an arm around Fulo's neck, bent him over. "No worries, mate. Drink will make it all the better."

This, everyone had to admit, made sense.

That's how the season started—at breakfast a week before our first race, under the cloud of the French driver's bad luck, with a bad decision to meet later that night at a bar on the bad side of Caracas.

Pricks of light glowed in the hills like sequins in a shroud. These were from the *ranchitos*, little cinderblock shanties stacked one on top of the other in mean neighborhoods surrounding the city. On the east side, drug dealers dealt their wares in the open. Sullen prostitutes beckoned from street corners. Uniformed cops, more scary than bandits, gnawed toothpicks and glared out from beneath shadowy doorways. The night was hot and smelled of city.

"Lovely," I said. "A truly lovely area."

"It has those South American atmospherics you admire so much, yeah, mate?"

DiCaprio shook his head. "Is like São Paulo, only not as nice," he said. "All for to feed your profound appetites for the alcohol."

"Our appetites are *profane*," Fulo said, "not profound." He had a hungry look in his eye. He said, "There it is, the place."

There it was all right. The bottom floor of a row of buildings surrounded by menacing alleys and unsavory foot traffic. A sign above the door read 'El Ratón' in downtown neon.

"The *Rat*?" I said. I gave a little laugh. "No doubt the name says it all."

"Correction," Fulo said. "*Ratón* means 'mouse.' The word for 'rat' is *rata*, you *gringo*. So you see your complaint has no basis in fact."

"You tell him," Rod said.

El Ratón was dark inside and smelled of mopped up booze and old cooking oil. Nothing eerie or sinister—not yet. Just normal Latin American weirdness. The empty dance floors were wide-planked, cut from hard, dark wood. Heavy carved tables squatted in the corners and black timbers spanned the ceiling—one of those strange, unexpected Bavarian interiors you found here and there across South America.

We took a back table beside a window looking on a bleak alley. We ordered a bottle of vodka, four glasses, orange juice.

"Remember," I said gravely, "beware of the ice."

Fulo smiled. "The Old Man has spoken."

We drank. Soon people were arriving: thin men in silk shirts, kinky women in tight dresses. A dwarfish emcee with one leg longer than the other mounted the stage to announce the band, which proceeded to inflict antique American Top 40 on us. The singer was a beauty contest has-been with ropes of hair to her waist. She belted out 'I Will Survive' in English, with whorish smiles and a heavy *carajita* accent. The dance floor filled up. Someone ordered another bottle.

Suddenly women were everywhere. DiCaprio's dark eyes scanned the dance floor slightly out of focus. His face was flushed. He was not used to keeping up with Fulo's drinking pace.

"It is the time," he said, "that we should be to making some of these girls feel the luckiness."

Fulo smiled and translated. "He wants to *fuck*!" he said. He swung his head with affection toward DiCaprio. He was pretty drunk himself. "You like to fuck, don't you, my friend?"

DiCaprio nodded, gazing off beyond Fulo's shoulder. They disappeared into the crowd.

"The children," Rod said, "are enjoying themselves."

Things were looking pleasantly blurry when Fulo and DiCaprio returned with a friend in tow.

"You have succeeded in finding no women," Rod said, "yet you have brought us this one swarthy young fellow."

"This is Mauricio," Fulo said. "You don't remember him?"

Mauricio turned out to be one of the local rich kids, a playboy who liked to hang around the drivers. I didn't like the type—their fathers occasionally bought them a place on a racing team. Sometimes they killed themselves or someone else. But Fulo knew he'd buy us drinks and so here he was. I sat back with my glass, annoyed, ignoring the fast Spanish and laughing.

Then Mauricio peered through the window beside our table and said something, laughed. He was looking through the window, where a small man—part Indian, part Creole, what the Venezuelans called *mestizo*—stood near a dumpster in the alley way. He was gazing through the window at the group of us, sketching something in a big tablet. He looked at us, sketched in the tablet, looked back at us.

Rod said, "What's this?"

DiCaprio looked. Fulo wanted to punch the guy in the nose.

Mauricio, the rich kid, told us to wait and disappeared through the front door. He reappeared a moment later in the alley. Mauricio glanced at the sketch, back in at us, and his head went back in a laugh. He was odd looking, this *mestizo*—long, gray hair pulled back in a ponytail, a lean face with one eye gone milky white. He didn't smile. Mauricio forked over a handful of *bolívares* and a few moments later was back at our table with a drawing—a caricature of DiCaprio, that had us all laughing out loud.

"A dead ringer, mates. Look at that mug!"

DiCaprio stared. The large ears, the turned-up nose, the too-pretty girlish face. It was him all right and then some, captured in that way caricature artists have. There was a sort of halo over his head above which the *mestizo* had scrawled some words in Spanish.

"What's this mean?" I asked.

Rod was looking at the words. "Well, it means something like: 'A long way from home this boy will have great luck.'" He deferred to Fulo who approved the translation with a shrug. "Whatever *that* means."

DiCaprio was laughing. "Is amazing!" he said. "How is he to know, this man, that I am perhaps far from home?"

Fulo said, "You talk like you're from another planet."

"Pal, he's really captured you," Rod said. "I gotta hand it to him."

Mauricio remained silent, pleased with himself. I looked for the old *mestizo* but now the alley outside was empty, filled only with strange green light.

I said, "He thinks you're lucky, DiCaprio. Maybe he didn't capture you all *that* well."

The band came and went. We drank more. Every now and then Di-Caprio pulled out the drawing so we could look at it. It kept us in good humor.

I was trying to calculate how much we had drunk when I felt Rod's elbow in my ribs. I looked up. On stage where the band had been there now stood a small, sway-backed pony. I shook my head, blinked but the animal remained. He regarded us with a forlorn expression, worldly, munching some hay that had been strewn around for him. Two teenage girls appeared on stage, a blonde and a brunette, junior Miss Venezuelas in Budweiser bikinis and stiletto heels.

"The plot," Fulo said, "thickens."

The little emcee took the microphone and began to talk. It became apparent that the emcee was none other than El Ratón himself. The Budweiser girls smiled enchantingly, El Ratón was howling. Mist curled from backstage.

At length we gathered that this was some kind of promotion. A bar contest, South American-style: Guess the horse's breed, win a door prize. The Venezuelans were forever picking up these North American gimmicks, then getting the details wrong, everything out of whack and a touch surreal. The room went nuts. People crowded the stage with slips of papers, rushing the girls. There was a big fishbowl on stage where they put the pieces of papers—chances—the room's conjecture concerning the breed of little horse we beheld. We wanted in on the action. Rod and Fulo feverishly translated, the rest of us scribbled horse breeds, along with our names onto little pieces of paper.

Ten minutes later, the girls drew DiCaprio's name from the fishbowl. We were on our feet applauding drunkenly. DiCaprio climbed the stage. The girls kissed him. El Ratón threw an arm over his shoulders, plunked a Bud hat on his head. They presented him with a wad of cash in a Budweiser envelope. The banners, the applause, the girls. It all brought to mind the winner's circle after a big race. DiCaprio beamed.

Back at the table, we slapped his back. Music started up, hot and loud.

"Why didn't you tell them we were drivers?" we asked.

DiCaprio looked at us. "I forgot!" he cried.

But the point wasn't lost on us. The artist, the *mestizo*, had been right about DiCaprio. He was a long way from home, and that night he was lucky.

Later we went singing into the crowded streets to go home. We looked for the *mestizo* to thank him but the strange little man was nowhere to be found.

We trained at *El Poliedro*. This was a hippodrome that had been converted years before into a grand prix race track. We spent afternoons
there running the cars, pushing them to their limits. Our crews were
local mechanics, car fanatics who worked double time for half pay. We
all dreamed of the same thing: glory. The Big Money. Kids hung around
El Poliedro watching from the stands. The whine of engines, the smell of
racing fuel, the hammering of pit tools—even in the Venezuelan heat,
these things brought us comfort.

Or that was the idea. I'm sure for the others—for Fulo the madman,
DiCaprio the kid, and for Rod my good friend—the practice runs were
relaxing. But lately in my own training I was seeing signs of The Fear. It's
something that can afflict drivers of a certain age, something everyone
knows about but never mentions. Coming into hard turns I lifted my
foot. I trail-braked when it wasn't really necessary behind other drivers and watched my side mirrors more than I had to. In the pits I made
excuses. The suspension felt loose. I couldn't hear the tires in the third
turn. I promised to push harder once the wings were adjusted just right.
The Fear. It makes you a menace on the course, dangerous to yourself and
other drivers. It makes you hesitate, and creates bad judgment. I didn't
breathe a word of this to anyone.

For a week we timed each other's laps. We talked about El Ratón,
how everyone loved the place. The guys talked about going back to see if
they could find the *mestizo*, get a little more good luck to rub off on us. I
sipped bottled water and held my tongue.

Qualifying was Saturday, timed laps to determine starting positions
for Sunday's opening race. Already they had dressed *El Poliedro* for the big
day. Banners flapped in the warm breeze; concessionaires had set up their
booths. Local journalists asked for interviews and the girls called out to
us as we passed by in racing suits.

Rod and I went to the pits and watched Fulo's qualifying run. He
exploded off the line. He screamed down straightaways and threaded
chicanes like there was no such thing as death. Rod shook his head. In
races Fulo relished the fishtail and oversteered for the joy of scaring op-
ponents away from his smoking rear tires. This form of madness has
its benefits. Fulo was a terror on the track. It was understood that if he
could tame this fearlessness, harness it, he would be unstoppable. If he
survived this phase of his career he might be great.

If. I held my breath and watched him slide toward a wall. White smoke
roiled from under the tires. He slid close enough to the concrete retainer

to leave a long black streak on a Valvoline ad. The crowd cheered. Rod said, "That boy worries me."

Fulo came into the pits, leapt from his car smiling. He said, "Great run, great run!"

Then DiCaprio left the starting line, the three of us watching. He drove as in a dream. Where Fulo relied on recklessness, DiCaprio was honing a sort of technical perfection. His car slipped into corners as if he had found invisible grooves on the track. He came out into straightaways with absolute control. Passing us on his fourth lap he raised his fist from the cockpit. Even before the official time, he knew he had won pole position for the race Sunday.

Fulo was jumping up and down. "The gypsy was right," he said. "DiCaprio has the luck, he has the luck!"

Even I had to admit it. The *mestizo* had read luck in DiCaprio's face earlier that week.

When DiCaprio took first place on Sunday we were convinced. The champagne, the local TV cameras and the girls in the victor's circle surrounding him? Who could deny it? That evening there were official celebrations to attend, bragging rights to be observed. It was the start of a great season, everyone agreed. A Mason Worldwide rep handed out cards at the post-race party, a huge potential sponsor, the big-time right there in the room beside us. We couldn't go to *El Ratón* that evening. But we decided we were going back all right. Just the four of us, as soon as possible, to see who the *mestizo*'s luck would rub off on next.

The four of us were packed into the little Fiat Fulo had bought. He darted up unfamiliar East Side streets and crossed wide congested avenues, no idea where he was going. Being lost, of course, made him drive faster. We flew past cars waiting at traffic lights and shot down narrow streets until we hit a barrio traffic jam. Then we weren't moving at all.

"Fuck *me*," Fulo said.

"Agreed," I said. "Fuck you."

In the daylight, the East Quarter was even uglier than before. Dirty hovels stared down malevolently from steeply raked hills. At street level aqua blue and flamingo pink facades sagged in the humidity. We crawled along. Heat and exhaust fumes filled the car. Kids stuck dirty fists in the windows demanding coins.

"I can't take this," Fulo said. He was sweat-slicked; hair was standing up in back where he'd been rubbing his head.

"You must not have to gotten lost," DiCaprio said.

Fulo gave him a look in the rearview. "I'm not lost," he said. "I'm just not sure where the fuck I am."

Ever calm, Rod said, "I think it's a few blocks over is all. We'll be there soon enough."

I smiled at Fulo's reflection in the rearview mirror. I said, "Look at him. Who does he look like."

Rod studied Fulo for a moment, then awareness dawned. "Fuck all, Fulo. Jack's right. I'm looking at Charlie Thorp."

I smiled. "Charlie *fucking* Thorp."

Fulo said, "Fuck you both."

We laughed. We explained to DiCaprio about Thorp. He was a driver on the circuit a few years before. He was one of those guys who talked endlessly about a wife and kid he had back in the States, told jokes that were so terrible they were funny. Everyone loved him, women especially. But he was never tempted by them. He fended them off with stories about his wife and some joke that had everyone crying with laughter. A good driver, too. But a little crazy.

I said, "Just thinking about that fucker makes me want to laugh."

Rod said, "Charlie Thorp. Haven't thought of him in, hell, I don't know how long."

Fulo drove the car up in the sidewalk to pass some traffic. People shouted and cursed at him from waiting cars. Fulo shouted back. Then there was another row of cars. Simmering in the distance was an intersection. We stopped again. Fulo said, "Christ, man." He shook his head. "Charlie. That was real fucked up, what happened."

"That it was, mate."

Fulo worked a muscle in his jaw and gripped the steering wheel tight.

"I remember like yesterday," Fulo said.

I said, "It's hot in here."

We sat silent for a while.

Rod said, "You were right there in the pits, weren't you, Fulo?"

Fulo shooed some kids away from the open window. "Right there, *cabrón*. In the pits."

"His wife and kid were there, remember?" I said.

"In the stands," said Fulo.

"Well, yeah, not in the fucking pits."

"He had bad tires. I told him, 'Don't do it, *cabrón*, just drop out. Don't fuckin' do it.' Raining. In fucking Monterrey."

I said, "It almost never rains there."

"It did that day."

"That was one shitty day," Rod said.

DiCaprio listened with a respectful smile.

"It was fucked up, all right," Fulo said

In a quiet voice, DiCaprio said, "Yeah, do you know? You might not to believe this but I sometimes am being scared. In cars."

Rod said, "Of course you are, mate. You'd be a fool not to be."

I stared out at a pile of rocks in front of a small building being torn down.

DiCaprio went on. "I mean, I never used to be doing this. But I enjoy it and so am worrying."

"Yeah, what about?"

DiCaprio frowned. "You know, man." The word sounded plural in his mouth—*men*. "The end of my life. I am worried about it happening. As I'm driving."

Rod frowned, displeased. "Yeah, well, that's the risk. But you don't talk about it, mate."

"Yeah, who brought this up anyway?" Fulo said. We were finally arriving at our turn to go through the intersection.

Rod slapped my shoulder. "The Old Man did. He's been downright morbid lately."

I shook my head very carefully. "Just thought of old Charlie Thorp," I said. "Nothing wrong with that."

We made a right turn and drove a short while in silence. There on the left was *El Ratón*. I was surprised by how it looked in the light. A dark, almost black front, smoke-stained, the color of a bruise. It sat there shimmering in the sunlight.

It was dark inside and quiet. A pair of men in suits were at the bar. The stage had drums set up, no musicians yet. We took our table by the window. Even at this hour the alley beyond it seemed cast in shadow. The waiter brought us mugs of 'hoppy hours' beer. Soon we were telling stories and avoiding topics like Charlie Thorp.

I went to the men's room. On my way I saw that the sun was already setting outside. A crowd was shuffling in. Back at the table Rod was looking into the alley. "Too bad our gypsy isn't here," he said, using Fulo's word for the *mestizo*. But for some reason I was relieved when I looked out into the empty alley.

After a few more beers the crowd was arriving and soon enough the band was playing again. One of the patrons recognized DiCaprio from the *Racing News*. People looked at us from their tables to see who he was.

Someone bought us a round of shots, then another. The band played a Brazilian song. Some girls had their picture taken with DiCaprio. One of them, dressed in chic black clothes and expensive jewelry, stayed behind. She was at least five years older than him. She sat on his lap. They spoke hybrid Spanish and Portuguese and giggled and gazed into each other's eyes.

We danced, some food got cold at the table. I went to the bathroom and when I came back, Rod asked over the loud music what time it was. I had to close one eye to see my watch clearly. I was shocked to see it was midnight.

"Well," Rod said with an odd smile. "Our friend is right on time."

There he was, standing in the green light in the alley, the *mestizo*, looking in at us, sketching in his big tablet again with a grease pencil. The same ponytail and strange, milky eye. I laughed with the others, full of bravado and cheap booze, encouraging him. He looked up occasionally from his pad. He never smiled, as if he were creating some great work of art, not a sketch of a bunch of drunks in a bar. The woman next to DiCaprio did not seem amused by what was going on.

DiCaprio said, "It seems to be creating you, Fulo, in the art."

Fulo was oddly quiet, watching the man with greedy eyes.

DiCaprio's girl pouted, watching as he went into the alley to buy the drawing. Back at our table she unrolled it so we could see. The drawing was all lips, big shoulders and thick wiry hair—Fulo, exaggerated, more like his face than any photo. In the drawing he was leaning up against a table, holding a cigar and leaning forward as if he were just about to tell you some funny story or punch your nose. It was a posture we all recognized. I laughed so hard that tears swam into my eyes.

In the corner the man had written *no seas loco, tenga cuidado*: stop being crazy, be careful. This just added to the hilarity.

Rod said, "He's fucking psychic!"

Fulo was still quiet. He stared at the drawing as if it hid the key to some amazing riddle.

The girl shivered. "Throw this thing away. It is not good to keep."

"You speak English!" I said.

She gave me a bored look. "Obviously." She sucked on a cigarette and regarded DiCaprio who was more interested in the sketch than in her. "These street people. I find them vile."

DiCaprio said, "He is friend of us, this little man."

The girl said, "He lives in *los ranchitos* in the hills."

Rod said, "He says our friend here is crazy, which he is."

As if that explained something.

"I can see that Fulo is crazy and I am not a psychic." She pointed toward the empty alley with her cigarette. "That man, he's trash."

This pretty much finished her with us.

It felt good to laugh. Just as last time, when we went looking for the little *mestizo*, he'd disappeared like a puff of smoke.

Fulo said, "Lucky Man, where you go? Lucky Man?"

And we laughed even harder when we realized Fulo was so drunk he couldn't remember where he parked the Fiat.

I couldn't sleep. I had a cheap apartment near Parque Central with a broken airconditioner and a hot-plate kitchen. But there was a small balcony with a decent view of the park. I stepped out onto it. It was hot, the kind of clinging heat that was going to last until morning. The park below was unlit and looked inky from here. You could hear kids shouting to each other from the darkness. Farther out the lights from the shantytowns glowed in the hills. I thought about life in those neighborhoods—short and brutal. This got me feeling depressed. I went back inside and paced. I was drunk. I tried to remember what the hell I was doing in Caracas. I picked up the telephone and then put it back in its cradle. If I had owned a TV I would have watched it. I picked up the phone again, dialed the country code for the States and then the number.

A woman's voice answered, groggy with sleep, my ex-wife, Karen.

When she heard my voice, she said, "Jack? What time is it? Is everything all right?"

I said, "Yeah, everything is fine."

Then I couldn't think of anything else to say.

"That's good." There was a silence. "Are you sure everything's all right?"

"I was just standing here, you know?" I fought to keep my words from slurring. "I got to thinking of you. I felt like calling. I guess I didn't bother to check the time."

We were married very young—I was younger even than DiCaprio. For a while it was fun. She came to my races in the States. She even followed me when I began to leave the country looking for easier sponsorship money and better fans. It's not much of a life for a married couple. I pictured Karen somewhere back in the States, squinting, up on her elbow, listening to her drunk ex-husband calling from another country with nothing much to say. I should have planned something to say.

I said, "A friend of mine, he just won a big race. I felt like talking to you."

"Are you there alone?" she asked.

"Oh, yes," I said. "Hey, remember Rod McCourt? He's down here this season."

"Right now?"

"No, I mean in Caracas with us."

There was another silence. "I don't think I remember him."

"Well, he's here."

"That's great," she said. "You're sure everything's okay?"

It went on like that for a little while longer. It was pretty bad. I said goodbye. I hung up and then went to bed. I lay there sweating and listening to the strange street from sounds below for a long time before I finally dozed off.

We were back to *El Poliedro* early the next afternoon. I still had booze fumes cooking in my head but this was an easy day, just a few laps for the mechanics. Rod's car was down and he was in the pit with his mechanics, joking with them in his slangy Spanish. I sat in the bay trying not to hurl. DiCaprio was at the track just relaxing.

But Fulo was on fire. He was convinced that the gypsy had conferred something special on him. He had the drawing tacked up in his car bay and was telling his teammates the story of where it had come from. He wanted to go out and run his car hard. There was no reason for this. He hadn't won the week before but he'd made a decent showing. We all had. Fulo should have just laid off. But no one felt like giving him advice he wasn't going to listen to anyway. He suited up and took his car onto to the track. As he walked away I thought of the *mestizo*'s words: don't be crazy, be careful. It got me chuckling to myself, thinking of that drawing.

He was doing wide sweeping ins and outs, hitting top speeds in the straightaways and swinging hard into turns. We half-watched, half-chatted in Rod's bay. I don't know where DiCaprio was. Fulo's car screamed past the pits, disappeared, then became visible again swinging left up onto the banked part of the oval. We watched and talked.

Fulo upped the speed. His pit boys loved it. I saw Rod looking and his mechanics watching. Fulo was running his car hard, the way only he could. He was fearless, driving for broke, like it was a race. He shrieked by, reappeared, and increased the speed.

A few fans were watching from the grandstands, on their feet and shading their eyes. In and out, in and out.

Rod and I looked up as Fulo came into the S-shaped turns near the grandstands. His car was shuddering the way it does when you drive too hard into a turn. To correct the skid, Fulo oversteered into the corner, allowing the rear of the vehicle to slip out of line with the front. The engine shrieked and made a strangling noise as he downshifted trying to slow. Sunlight flashed once from the top of his helmet like a beacon.

"Oh, fuck," Rod said.

I've crashed into the wall half-a-dozen times. Any driver has. What you remember later is this: it *hurts*. You see it coming not exactly in slow motion but more as if you're watching it happen to someone else, the way you'd feel if you saw a man on a tall scaffolding about to give way. You can see what's going to happen ahead of time and there's not a damn thing you can do to stop it. Then *bam*. Your wrists snap, the force jars your body, your ribs pop. Your teeth hurt for a week.

This had happened to me. But I had never crashed like Fulo did on this practice run. It was the kind of crash you see on TV or in video clips. Later people said it looked like Fulo had *tried* to drive into the wall but that was untrue. I saw him trying to correct the slide. For a moment white smoke from the tires obscured everything. There was the loud shout of metal twisting. There was a fireball and smoke. The safety cage flew from the smoke cloud tumbling down the straightaway with Fulo still inside. We ran across the field toward what was left of the car.

The ambulance crew pulled Fulo from the dented safety cage. They claimed he was still alive but he didn't look it. His limbs were twisted into strange shapes, the Kevlar suit singed all over and shredded in places. Black skin streaked with red showed through. His helmet was dented. I was sent running to get something from his locker. The crew stood there in the bay, not knowing what to do. On the wall was the picture from the night before, the one drawn by the gypsy.

I said, "Will somebody take this fucking thing down!" and pulled it from the wall in front of our stunned crew.

Fulo was alive but barely. The Venezuelan doctors said he might wake up, he might not, they didn't know. He would lose an arm, they said. It was funny how little we actually knew about him. I knew he was from Miami. But I didn't know whether he had brothers or sisters, for instance. Someone managed to track down a relative and make a call back to the States. Fulo's family was contacted. They called back.

DiCaprio was the one who ended up speaking with them. Fulo's family, it turned out, had a lot of money.

"They are rich," DiCaprio said.

"What?" I said.

"He is quite rich," DiCaprio said. "With money."

Standing there by the bed in the hospital, it made us feel better to think Fulo's family had money that he had never bothered to mention.

"He was holding out on us," Rod said. "This fucking madman."

Fulo's parents and a sister arrived. They weren't much interested in us. We were just another part of the problem, I suppose. Fulo's mother held his hand and kept saying, "Why would you do this to yourself? Why would you do this?"

It was decided that Fulo was going back to the States for treatment. The Venezuelan doctors agreed, relieved to have the mess off their hands. Fulo's parents arranged a fixed-wing ambulance back to Miami. They were loaded. His family was cordial to us, though they disliked and partly blamed us. His sister was fat, not very pretty, but nicely dressed the way rich people are. Fulo had no say in the matter. He went on sleeping like a one-armed baby with a puffy face.

We told him goodbye at the hospital. They rolled him away, unaware, and loaded him into a car to take him to the airport. That was the last we saw of Fulo.

It was decided that the team would go ahead and keep racing. We said that's how Fulo would have wanted it. We had another race in less than a week's time.

Right away Rod started working on me to go back to El Ratón. He wanted to see what the gypsy had to say about one of us—about him or me. He said it with a hard glint in his eye, a challenge. DiCaprio remained silent when he brought it up. We were at my apartment. It had turned oddly cool that night. The door to my balcony was open, it was dark.

I said no fucking way was I going back to that place. I told him I didn't like to drink this close to a race. I told him I didn't believe in any of that shit, anyway.

"Then what's the harm? Let's just go, sit around and sip soda water. We don't have to drink."

"I told you, no fucking way."

Rod and I were friends from before Caracas—but he wouldn't get off my back. "Jack, if there's nothing to this shit, then go back. You said it yourself. It's not real, anyway."

"No."

Rod's face went stony. "What are you afraid of, mate? Huh? A little old man? He's a fucking street vendor for fucking tourists. He makes funny little drawings. You think he's psychic? Then let him read the fucking future for us. If he isn't, then no harm done. It's a game. What difference does it make whether or not he's for real?"

"You wanna know what's for real, Rod? Fulo is a vegetable getting fed and watered somewhere in Miami with a tube up his ass. And Charlie Thorp is dead. That's for real."

DiCaprio said, "Come on...."

Rod ignored him. "Whatever you're afraid of, it's all in your head, mate. It's all up in that fucking head of yours." He looked at me hard. There was a pause. Then he said, "Don't be a fucking coward. We're going."

They were looking at me. There was a squeaking noise and a little bat from the park flitted stiffly into the living room, dazed by the light. That sort of thing happened all the time and we hardly noticed. It banked here and there like a giant bug, confused, then found its was back out into the night.

"You want to go back to the bar? Fine. Let's go. Right now."

"Let's go, then."

DiCaprio rolled his eyes.

"Then let's go."

There was a cool breeze filled with imminent rain. This was strange weather for Caracas and felt like fall back home. It was late when we arrived at the *El Ratón*.

There was the regular crowd. No one paid much attention to us. If they'd heard about Fulo a few weeks ago, they weren't showing it. At the table it was strange without him, as if he'd just gotten up for a piss and would be back to start a fight with someone at the next table in a minute or two. But Fulo wasn't coming back.

The waitress gave us a strange look when we ordered soda water. When she realized we were serious, she shrugged and went off for it. We listened to the music and didn't speak much to each other.

Between songs we heard the wind outside. Rain swept through the alley and dripped from an overhand. But the gypsy was nowhere to be seen.

After another round of soda water and a trip to the bathroom I declared it time to leave. DiCaprio agreed.

Rod wanted another round.

I said, "What are you trying to prove? We came, like you wanted. Nothing happened. Let's go."

Rod stared out the window. Rain licked through the alley. He got out his wallet and started counting out bills.

DiCaprio said, "Look, into the window."

The little *mestizo* had appeared. He wore a hoodless poncho, his hair plastered to his skull. He stood in a triangle of green light, rain spitting behind him. From a plastic bag he removed his drawing pad. He began his trick, glancing up occasionally with his one good eye as he sketched.

We sat there, no longer laughing. Why had he singled us out? Or maybe Rod was right, maybe that was in my head, too. The little *mestizo*, of course, went from table to table, a step up from begging, to sell his coarse drawings. Of course, we just happened to be the only ones interested in them. Of course.

When he finished he waved at DiCaprio to come out. DiCaprio got up slowly, glancing at me.

Rod said, "Hurry up. The guy's standing in the rain."

I said, "Are you having fun?"

Rod ignored me. He watched DiCaprio pay the guy. When he came back in chilly wind followed him. The unexpected smell of autumn made me think of home.

In the drawing Rod and I slouched in our seats, relaxed—big heads and little bodies, a cartoon. My arm was slung over Rod's shoulder and we appeared to be in a reflective mood, as if we'd been caught mid-conversation on some matter of interest or importance.

Above us the *mestizo* had scrawled the words, "Beware the dangerous season."

No one laughed.

Finally, DiCaprio said, "It does not appear like the two of you anyway."

"The dangerous season," I said. I was looking at the picture so I wouldn't have to look at Rod.

"Whatever it means," Rod said again, "it's in your head."

By race day a hot spell had settled in for good. We watched the weather and on race morning we made the decision to put dry surface tires on the car—no treads, wide, fat tires. Each turn gave me butterflies, which I wrote off to pre-race jitters. The race was being televised: Televisión Caracas and ESPN-2 were there. An Argentinean reporter I knew asked whether she could have a pre-race interview with me in my practice suit. I wet my hair, slicked it back with her comb. She interviewed Rod next. We hadn't spoken all week. England and Spain had crews there. This was a big race and Rod for one was hoping to use it for a jump to the big leagues.

I walked around the car, talked with my mechanics, then went to take a shower. I had just put on my racing suit and was ready to go back to the paddock when Rod walked up to me.

He stuck out his hand. "With that suit on, you look almost like a race car driver."

I shrugged, shook his hand. I said, "Best of luck. Mate."

He winked. "Let's make it a winning season."

The heat was incredible. I put on my helmet. We climbed into our cars, all lined up behind the pole and started the engines. The temperature climbed in the cockpit and soon there was that feeling—heat in your face, crawling up your body. Waiting with your legs stretched out to the clutch and accelerator, back jammed against the seat, two feet off the ground. Girls with short skirts were positioned by each of the cars holding umbrellas over the pilots to keep the sun from baking down on our heads. It didn't help much. At the fifteen minute warning a guy looking down into the viewer of an ESPN-2 TV camera came walking slowly down the line of cars.

He walked toward me. My crew chief stepped back. The legs of the girl holding the umbrella did their little model's stance for the camera. I did what was expected—held my thumb in the air, nodded, then looked away, bored by it all. Cocky, fearless driver. Fulo floated into my mind and the ghost of Charlie Thorp. I doubted whether the little *mestizo* had a TV but I wondered: did he watch the races on it if he did? The crowd leapt when we took our first lap, swinging back and forth, to warm up the tires and ease our nerves.

Then we were back at the line. Time to race. I banished all thought except the starting line from my mind.

The starting light went off. In front of me I could see the polesitter was having a problem—he wasn't taking off like he should and right away Rod's black car jumped out in front of him. I found myself surprised as I followed his line and that fast we were in first and second place with the polesitter finally coming out behind us. I slid in behind Rod, trying to find a groove, saying to myself: just like practice, just like practice. We ran one, two, three of the five mile laps like this. I tried occasionally to slip inside on a turn, pass Rod, but he was watching me, swinging tight on turns, holding me back. In my mirror I saw DiCaprio do the same thing behind me.

Rod was pushing our speed. He charged into turns, cut the tangent hard into a chicane and then swung out to block me. I wanted to pass him worse than I had ever wanted anything before. I was furious with wanting to pass him. But each time we charged into a turn at these speeds my stomach tightened. I felt just at the edge of control. Sweat got into my eyes, and I was blinking.

Behind me I saw a puff of white smoke—something shot past me, and I realized DiCaprio had just spun off the course. His day was over.

It was Rod and me. I was trying to get around him, somehow take the lead. He was my friend, but I was working up an anger at him, a fury—that thing you needed that pushed you to pass someone at these kinds of speeds on the tight confines of a grand prix course. I tried to pass around the outside of turns, almost made it, then got cut off again. All I saw was the rear spoiler and huge open tires of Rod's car ahead of me, the dangerous open tires, and an idea came into my head. As we plunged into a wide turn that took us near a wall, I decided to fake outside, then go inside the turn. Rod would move to keep me blocked outside, and then I could pass him even though I was going slightly slower. It was a risky strategy. But I was furious. I was scared. I wanted to prove something. I didn't want to lose. For a fleeting moment Fulo and Charlie Thorp were in my mind. I said to myself, fuck them and fuck Rod. I faked right, plunged inside and started to race past Rod.

Joy leapt up inside of me. I was passing him. I'd tricked him. Rod glanced my way. No face, just the blank mirror of his mask as the helmet turned my way—as if he were startled by this daring move, interested in my odd strategy.

Accidents happen fast at speed. I was almost past Rod, taking the lead, when a puff of white smoke appeared in my right mirror. Rod disappeared behind fog and I wondered where it had come from. Then there was a terrific noise, the road came up and slammed into me, then slammed into me again. It felt like I couldn't breathe, like my legs were breaking off. I wanted to cry. I wanted my mother. Then it was calm, the crisis was past, and the fog became air again and I breathed.

A long stay in a foreign hospital changes you. There was a period where everything was strange. Hundreds of faces looking down at you, a weird language you can't understand. You seem to recognize everyone. I saw people looking at me all the time. I had this recurring dream: every day they came in to peel my skin from me. I was swaddled in shrouds. Then one day the pain from my burns woke me up and I saw people around. There were DiCaprio and a couple of other guys we knew from the race circuit in the room.

Karen was in the room with me and so was Rod. Everyone speaking, laughing, and though I couldn't speak to them, I could see and hear them and was comforted. The pain from my burns was maddening. I wanted pain killers all the time. Faces hovered. There was the loneliness of long nights when I knew my body was broken. There was the oddity of knowing I'd changed.

One day I was awake and the doctors made me stand up. I had a tube up my dick and walked like an old man with feeble arms of loose skin held out to the sides.

Burns climbed up my back and chest and in the mirror I saw that scars licked up under my jaw. I had the face of an ancient man. On the back of my head some hair was gone for good, they told me.

I asked where Karen was, and Rod and DiCaprio, but the nurses didn't understand me well—and when they finally did, they said they didn't know these people.

Finally DiCaprio came with his rich friend, Mauricio. They sat with me sipping sparkling water. I asked him about Karen and he said I must have been dreaming because as far as he knew she'd never come.

I asked about Rod.

DiCaprio told me he had not been to visit me, and looked away.

"He was here, DiCaprio. I saw him. In this room, after the accident."

"We are not to speak of this," he said. And quickly left the room.

It was Mauricio who told me what had happened at the race. As I passed Rod that day, trying to turn back in front of him, the rear right tire of my car had touched the front left one of his. It's the first thing you learn: stay away from the open wheels. They spin at different speeds and if one of your tires touches the spinning tire of another car the torque can launch you right into the air. This is what happened to me. My car took off, caught in the wind, and sailed back onto Rod's car, a spectacular crash. The cars had been sandwiched together by the force of the accident, fused in parts, and burned. And Rod? He had never stood a chance.

I sat, absorbing the news that was weeks and weeks old for everyone else but new and painful to me.

When DiCaprio returned, he was angry with Mauricio for telling me. But I said it was all right—had they planned never to tell me?

DiCaprio just sort of nodded and looked away from me, the way people did.

When I left the hospital I went back to the track just once. When the new attendant realized who I was, he helped me onto the course, showed me where the accident had occurred. I'd never met him but he knew who I was. He told me he'd seen the tapes of my crash—he crossed himself, folded his thumb and index finger into a cross to kiss. It was, he said, *un milagro* that I was even alive.

Rod and I spoke under the spreading shadow of a great tree like the ones we have back home. Whether it was in a dream or simply a ghost, I can't be sure.

I asked what he had thought of my maneuver to cut him off—whether it was the right thing to do, or a hotdog move, ungentlemanly. He smiled slightly, but didn't respond.

"I was afraid," I told him. "Of the speed, of losing. I was afraid."

"No one blames you," he said finally. "There are risks. It's not your fault."

I left Caracas early in October. DiCaprio took me to the airport and there wasn't much to talk about. I didn't mention racing, the dangerous season, or Rod. I was thinking of home—the red and yellow leaves of fall, cool Ohio air.

DiCaprio waited as I got ready to board the plane. He said, "Who is to pick you up when you are getting home?"

I told him I didn't know.

He said, "You must call, to keep touch."

I promised. I wished him luck and told him I'd keep up with his career.

My flight was called and DiCaprio hugged me carefully not to hurt me where I had been burned. I turned and made my way to the plane that was waiting to take me back.

Almost Home

Denise Pierce was held up in Bang-kok because of an August storm in the Philippines and so nearly missed her connection from Taipei to Los Angeles. This was how things worked at the beginning of the new century.

She struggled down the aisle of the plane. The L.A. flight was always completely full, a misery. But she was flying business class so they'd held her spot. *Run*, they told her at the gate, and she had, up the weirdly slop-ing concourses at Chiang Kai-Shek Airport, wheelie bags in tow, barely making the flight. Now she was slick with sweat, wet like something drowned. Behind her a flight attendant closed the forward door. A vacu-um–hiss sealed them in.

She found an overhead bin for her bags (they were heavy, no one of-fered help) and then went in search of her seat. She found it, a window seat about halfway down the business class cabin, the only open spot left in the compartment. Between it and her sat a pink-faced man with a belly that belonged on a pregnant woman.

"Sorry," she said, offering a small smile in apology.

He had to stand to let her in. He pursed his lips, tucked his newspaper under his arm and struggled to his feet. The belly pressed against her backside as she passed by.

Denise sagged into her seat. The tarmac outside was a boiling black lake in the rain, the outside world painted in broad streaks of light.

"Excuse me." Denise turned to see her seat partner's pink face. "Do you realize that they held the plane up for you?"

"Pardon me?"

He spoke with the sort of drawl that brought to mind big steaks and dustbowls. "I just wondered if you realized they held it up for you. We all had to wait."

"Somehow I doubt they held the plane for me. They don't do that."

"If you had been on time, we'd already be up in the air."

She smiled, showing teeth. "I doubt it."

A voice spoke over the intercom, the cabin lights dimmed, and then they were in the sky. The fancy business class seats had little foldout screens in the middle armrest—Denise turned hers on to watch their plane's progress over a little map of the world. Familiar cities studded the Asian continent like seeds in bread: Sapporo, Osaka, Wuhan, Quezon City, and further back, Bangjou, Pusan, Shanghyang, Taegu, Tianjin. How many of these places had she been to? In five years she'd visited almost all of them, for a day at least. A solitary melancholy crept over her as these places receded into her past. She anticipated many reflective hours on the flight. For the first time since packing she had time to think. "Five years!" she thought.

A flight attendant appeared offering drinks. She had vaguely Cantonese features but spoke with a delicate Mandarin accent.

The man beside her wanted bourbon and Diet Coke. "We call that a trailer park Manhattan lite back home," he guffawed.

The young woman responded with a bland smile and said, "Do you take ice?"

"What?"

"Ice?"

"Oh, yeah, I want some ice!"

Denise asked for red wine. "*Shie shie,*" she said, accepting.

This time the woman's smile was the real thing. An American replying in Mandarin was a rarity, Denise knew.

She opened a book.

"You Oriental?"

The scrubbed face was turned her way again.

"Pardon me?"

"Oriental. The way you spoke there with that stewardess. That and your, you know, your eyes."

"No, I'm not Asian," she said.

"No offense." He sipped his drink. "Going home, eh? Me too." He leaned toward her with a smile. "It sure feels good to be getting back to civilization. Good old US of A. What are you, a student? A boyfriend living over in Japan or something?"

Living overseas she'd cringed when other Americans said and did incredible things. Couples in Bermuda shorts strolling straight into a temple with sneakers on and white socks. She'd seen a grown man, an angry American businessman, mimic a young bellman with monkey noises in the Hotel Sofitel to express displeasure. Denise would be appalled and then a colleague, usually a European, would make some cutting joke and she would become protective—angry even. This man beside her wore a starched white shirt over his bulging belly. A plastic runner's watch was strapped to his soft wrist. Here was a stereotype wrapped in a cliché, slurping his trailer park Manhattan lite, that simple complex thing—an American.

"I *work*, actually," she said, "as a journalist." She named the magazine she wrote for, which often had the effect of shutting people up.

"Mainstream media," he said with a chuckle. "You ever get to meet Rush Limbaugh? I did, once."

Denise went back to her book.

They were somewhere over the Sea of Japan. Most of the passengers in the cabin had unfolded their little TV screens and plugged their heads into earphones to stare at a rerun of some American sitcom, *Seinfeld,* she guessed. Laughter exploded around her at irregular intervals. The man beside her was beached in his seat, a brain-dead smile on his face. He popped mixed nuts into his mouth and stared at the screen as if it contained the answer to some great riddle. He laughed whenever the others did, rats in a mad scientist's experiment. He wiggled his stockinged toes whenever he laughed, Denise noticed with distaste.

What was it about him that grated so much? In Asia she'd come to understand how well she had lived her entire life. On her first assignment in Manila, she'd driven a cameraman, a professional man eight or ten years her senior, to his home, a one-room cinderblock box he shared with his entire family in the shadow of a glass and steel tower; the man's wife had forced Denise to take fruit before she'd left. In a village outside of Kiashung she covered a flood with a film crew and watched in horror as a small boy was whisked away in racing brown water, his head bobbing like a cork before disappearing. The boy's father dived into the water and disappeared after him. It seemed to her that somehow these people paid for the glass towers in cities around the world.

Food smells filled the cabin and soon flight attendants were bumping around behind metal carts. When they arrived at Denise's row, the well-fed man beside her raised his seat and examined the cart with wolfish eyes.

Denise chose the Asian meal and another glass of wine. Her seatmate was munching on salad and the second of three rolls he'd required.

He glanced over at Denise, who had unfurled a pair of chopsticks and had begun to eat Shu Mai with pickled soy.

"You work those sticks pretty good," he said. "I never learned it. But then again, I'm not crazy about the food over here. Something just plain weird about it." To his sophisticated palette the man raised bourbon and Diet Coke. He told her he sold refrigerator elements and traveled several times a year to service the Asian account. He took up his knife and fork and spoke without looking up from his steak. "Heard a scary story while I was over here this time. These Chinese. Maybe it's something you can use in your paper."

Denise didn't reply, the man not so much talking to her as just talking.

"Friend a mine, guy works for one of the car companies, one of the Big Four, told me about it, living there over in Beijing, you know? Jesus Christ, Beijing. Anyway, he's been working out there, I don't know— what?—couple a years anyway, really likes it too, I guess. Go figure. Well, this guy knows another guy who just moved out recent, few months ago, transferred over for the company. He brought his wife and little girl over with him, too. Expats." He said the word as if it tasted bad in his mouth. "I couldn't have done that to my kids when they were little."

He looked over to see whether Denise was paying attention and some instinct—politeness or a reporter's willingness to listen to any story— made her nod.

"So the little girl's having serious trouble adjusting. It's a normal American little kid—I mean, who the hell *wouldn't* have trouble? I start to lose it myself after more than a week over here. So the mother and father, they're all concerned. Little girl isn't eating right, she's withdrawn, you know—not talking much. So they decide to take her downtown and go shopping. There's a sort of an area up there of shops and food places. It's Chinese but it's a change."

Denise knew the area he was talking about, she said.

"Yeah, anyway this little girl's all sad and so there they are walking along when they come up to a booth where this little Chinese guy's selling puppies and the kid, she brightens up right there on the spot, you can see her mood change right away, she's all happy and excited. And her parents, you know, it's the first time they've seen the kid smile in weeks. So she's petting the little pooch—it's *real* cute, I guess—and it's licking her face and jumping on her, and the parents are telling the guy—he doesn't speak English, of course—'This one, this is the one she wants, how much for this one here?' and they somehow get across that they want to buy her the puppy. They pay for it and tell him they're gonna look around a little more, and will he hang on to the dog till they get back?"

Here he leaned in toward Denise to deliver the kicker for full impact. "So guess what happens when they come back."

Now Denise leaned toward him. "The man hands the little girl a paper butcher's bag and says, 'Here's your dog, all ready to go.'"

The man blinked, his scrubbed face expressing surprise. "You already heard about it?"

Denise shook her head, taking wicked pleasure in pricking the big balloon of a man. "*Everyone's* heard it. It's just a made-up story."

The man placed a piece of bread absently in his mouth. "I don't know," he said, suddenly less sure of himself. "This guy who told me about it, you know, he knows the family it happened to. I guess it really messed the little kid up."

"Give me a break. It's an urban legend. It never really happened."

"Well, I don't know." He wore a pensive look, chewing his bread. "You've probably seen some things with your job out here, I bet."

"Some." None of which Denise cared to share with this man. She gave a saccharin smile. "I have to go to the restroom," she said. "Do you mind?"

But he was right. She had seen plenty of things—strange, sad, funny, horrifying things. She retook her seat and let her mind wander to trips made in northern China when *she* had worked out of Beijing, the little restaurants and their hilarious attempts to translate menus into English: the special at one mom and pop shop had been 'chicken with skeleton pulled out.' She would publish a book of these mistranslations back home, she told her friends, one of a million things that would never happen. Denise had left the States thinking she was grown up, tough. When her grandmother died just before the New Year, Denise skipped the funeral; she had been assigned to cover the millennium celebrations in Hong Kong, she explained; there was nothing she could do. Her own grandmother. Denise had seen suffering in Asia that made the grief of one family, even hers, seem like an indulgence. She suspected her own Western wealth was carried on narrow, Asian shoulders.

People liked to blame Americans for everything, a favorite pastime that Denise herself occasionally enjoyed. She had been based in Taipei in the heyday of the Tiger Economies. One story she covered there was of an American contractor sent from the States for Mason Worldwide. It was the ultimate low-profile, high-profit multinational conglomerate—and happened to be the company her own father had worked for and which currently employed her younger brother. This man, Schuman, had been sent to rationalize the company's wireless operations. "I'm gonna fix business where it's broke," he'd told her in their first interview, "and leave it alone where it ain't."

His speech was vulgar but his office was wainscoted in rare cherry wood and he wore French cuffs and tailored suits. A dusting of gray on his temples lent him an air of probity and power but he couldn't have been more than forty. He announced a plan to shut down more than half of the retail phone outlets in the island, gray-market shops, very Chinese, that were costing the company marginal profits. Did he worry, she wondered, that many people would suffer? He believed this would be true in the short term but that things would be better for everyone in the long run—that all-American answer. She had also asked about threats he'd received for his plan—most of these dealers were under the control of very ruthless organized criminals, after all. He waved her questions off, laughing. They wouldn't fuck with an *American* company, he said. She had disliked him and his easy dismissals, his sense of entitlement. She knew his type.

And yet. One day she met him for an interview in his refrigerated office and he waved his arms. "I'm hungry," he announced, "let's go to the Old Lady's." And she followed him outside to the steaming alleys behind the glimmering World Trade Center building in Taipei. He'd loosened his tie in the dizzying heat and walked through the street throng, past the gold jeweler and the shop where men had their tailored shirts made and led her to the noodle shop known among the expats as the Old Lady's. The old lady in question yelled at the patrons, a sour looking old hag, and the food served there was real Chinese. And this man, Schuman, who she'd thought of as the epitome of the ugly American, he ate fiery noodles and downed the thick smoky soy drink that gagged Denise herself. He joked in very bad Taiwanese with the Old Lady herself, who had obvious fondness for the white man. Denise had been jolted by this humanness—a lesson. She had been gone a few months, assigned to Bangkok, when she heard the news that Schuman had been gunned down by thugs in front of his family at his condo in Taipei. She had been shocked at the stupid brutality of it, of everything, and then was surprised by her own capacity to be shocked.

It was nighttime. The plane was dead silent now. Around her people slept; the flight attendants were nowhere to be seen. Someone a few rows over was snoring like a buzzsaw. The light in the plane had a weird bluish tint to it and for some reason she was transported to her childhood home. She half expected her mother to come walking up the aisle, a younger version of her brother bounding behind. Denise was going on from L.A. tomorrow to New York City where she had accepted an important editorial job for her slick magazine. She would be staying with friends and looking for an apartment in Manhattan and would visit her family at Christmas, if at all. She had expected a dose of culture shock. But what she hadn't expected was this collision of past and present, the disorientation of five years gone. Her country would be five years changed, her friends had moved five years on with their lives and she felt somehow frozen in place where she left. Only now her grandmother was dead, her brother living in another state. What she hadn't expected was to feel so homesick when she was almost home.

Denise was trapped in the detestable window seat and so, of course, had to pee again. The man beside her had reclined his seat and lay motionless now. She hoped the bathroom urge might be in her head, something that would go away. The man beside her had left his little screen out and it was playing the same rerun of the same sitcom as earlier. Sickly shadows flickered over his face. The headphones had slid around his throat from where they emitted tinny sounds. His rimless glasses were still in place; the screen light reflected in the lenses gave him the eerie look of an eyeless sea creature.

Denise began moving things around in her seat in preparation of standing. She folded her seat tray loudly, hoping the commotion would wake him up. He slept like a sack. She cleared her throat and considered turning on the light. But there were the other innocent passengers around to think about.

She cleared her throat more loudly. Nothing.

She was going to have to wake him up. "Hey," she whispered harshly. "Hey. Excuse me."

The man's face remained slack.

"*Pssst*. Hey, you. Come on." Reluctantly, she reached out to touch his spongy shoulder She pushed harder. "Ex*cuse* me."

Suddenly she wasn't sure the man was breathing. He'd tugged a blanket halfway up his belly and the light pouring from the screen rippled over him, making it hard to tell what was moving and what wasn't. But this was a big, fat man and it shouldn't have been hard to tell whether he was breathing. Denise recalled the anecdote of a stateside colleague in which a friend of a friend told of a man dying beside him on an overnight flight. According to the story, the plane had been completely full and there was nothing for the man to do but sit there next to the corpse till the plane landed. Denise had always assumed that the anecdote was as fake as the puppy-butcher story. But Denise was tired, the cabin was bathed in unearthly light and she felt it with creepy certainty: *this man isn't breathing!*

Now she definitely didn't want to touch him. She thought about ringing a flight attendant but imagined herself trapped in the seat while passengers watched and crewmembers tried to decide what to do with the oversized corpse at her side. Denise felt a steady beat of panic starting. She looked around. A lone light burned way up at the front of the cabin. Except for that, the entire cabin seemed dead.

"Hey," she hissed. She poked him with her book. If he wasn't dead, he was the soundest sleeper she'd ever seen. His feet were sticking under the seat in front of him, there was no way she could get through, and now the bathroom thing was getting urgent; she needed to get free.

Denise was small and kept herself fit; the answer, when it occurred to her, seemed reasonable enough. She undid her seatbelt and sat up. She put one hand firmly on the console between the seats, then gently eased herself over, past the man's TV screen, toward the aisle. She cantilevered her left leg and inched carefully above the man's belly, facing him; like someone descending a dark stairwell, she extended her toe, hoping to feel solid aisle beneath. The man made no move.

She eased her leg further over, holding her breath, straddling the man. She had nearly cleared the seat when she slipped and collapsed, straight down, hard—and lay sprawled, like a lover, across the man's vast belly.

Well, she could tell that he was breathing now, his breath warm and boozy on her face. Behind rimless lenses the man's eyes opened and gazed into hers. For a long time she was unable to gain purchase and lay like a butterfly with pinned wings. She struggled to get her hands back on the arm rests to lever herself off, the man watching wordlessly up into her eyes the entire time.

"My God, I'm so sorry," she mumbled, "I had to, I, it was—I'm sorry—" finally she managed to push off and out into the aisle. She scurried to the bathroom, cursing under her breath.

When she returned the man's seat was empty. He was nowhere to be seen—must have gone off to a bathroom himself or for a stroll through coach class. Denise slipped into her seat and pulled a flimsy in-flight blanket over her head and turned, mortified, toward the window.

The smell of food filled the cabin again. Denise blinked her eyes open. Looking at the shade covering the window beside her was like facing the sun with your eyelids closed. A riot of warmth and light burned at the edge of the shade. What time was it? What *day* was it? It was impossible to tell and her watch was in her bag. Denise could never remember: did you fly from night into day when you flew eastward or the other way around?

She sat up and remembered the man beside her like a bad dream.

"Good morning," he said. He had righted his seat and unfolded the seat tray. "Did you sleep well?"

She sat up and adjusted the blanket in her lap. "Fine, thank you."

"Did you have strange dreams?" He sipped coffee. "I sure did."

"I'm sorry," she said, "but I need to use the restroom."

"*Again?*"

She smiled in fury. "Do you mind?"

When she returned the flight attendant was in the aisle with a puzzled look in her eye and the fat man was laughing.

"Tell her what's in the Asian breakfast," the man said as Denise passed to her seat. It was a different woman from the night before.

"I say congee come for Asian breakfast," the woman said in broken English.

"And what's in it?"

"Congee," she said, trying to be polite. She explained it was made with rice, the R struggling not to become an L in her mouth.

"*Lice!*" The man laughed and brought his hand down on his sausage-like thigh. "That's an Asian breakfast for you, all right. Lice and eggs!"

The stewardess looked at Denise quizzically and then back at the man, a innocent smile on her lips. She tried again to explain then gave up. She said breakfast would arrive soon and retreated down the aisle.

"She meant rice," he said, chuckling. "Lice...."

She thought of the man in the Hotel Sofitel mimicking the desk clerk. Finally, *finally,* she rose to his bait. "You know something," she said. "You're an asshole."

"Pardon me?"

"I said, you're an *ass*hole. You remind me of every big, fat, loudmouth American I've seen in the last five years, in my whole life!"

He set his cup down and leaned forward. "It was the way she said it, you see. It sounded funny to me."

"You speak one language. Barely. That woman speaks at *least* two."

"Yeah. And *she's* serving *me* coffee."

Denise tossed her arms up in amazement. "You come to *her country* to sell refrigerator parts! And *you* make fun of *her*? Asshole!"

"You don't really like me very much, do you?"

"Duh!"

He wore a gross little grin. Denise was surprised by his composure—but then here was a man who was probably accustomed to being called an asshole.

"You didn't like me since the second you sat down, big college-educated girl. Well, let me tell you something, lady. We're more alike than you wanna think, you and me."

"Don't bet on it."

"You think your fancy newspaper would even *send* you over here if people like me weren't out selling things. It's business that makes the world go around, honey. It's selling things to these people that bought you your nice business class seat and your ticket home. You're just selling something, too."

"You think that gives you a right to make fun of people, to be cruel to them to their face?"

He shrugged. "Who's being cruel? She was having a good time. It sounded funny is all." He chuckled again at the memory. "*Lice.*"

"It's people like you who give us all a bad name. People like you make people like her hate all of us."

But he sat back, in blissful ignorance. He sipped his coffee. On a metal cart a Denver omelet was being trundled his way by people he made fun of. "One day," he said, "you'll see. You'll understand we're more alike than we're not."

"Dream on, mister."

"Hell, after last night, we're practically family."

Denise slammed open her window shade and stared out at the vast sea below. Scalloped waves were a million unruly mirrors reflecting the sun. Denise was determined not to speak to the man for the rest of the flight—never to speak to him again, if she could help it.

They were descending toward L.A., which lay sprawled beneath in a brownish haze. Denise was almost home. She had opened a book and not spoken a word to the man beside her; when she'd had to go the bathroom she held it till he got up, and she hurried back to beat him to the seat. Now she watched through the window as the landscape of home tipped and tilted then finally righted itself. It was late August, hot down there. She would be going on later in the afternoon to New York City, for a new job, a new life.

The plane taxied in and stopped, and now there was chattering and excitement on the airplane as people stood, stretched their legs, began retrieving their bags, the conclusion of a routine jaunt from half a world away. She did her best to ignore her seat mate before escaping the plane. When he bade her goodbye, she busied herself with her things and pretended not to hear. His chuckle followed him up the aisle and out of her life.

A flight attendant and pilot waited by the door with insincere fare-wells. Denise smiled back and it hit her, she didn't even really know what day it was. She asked the flight attendant who smiled, told her: August 10th.

She walked down the jetway. August 10, 2001! It was too early to tell how it felt to be back. In the swarm of people outside of customs, she caught sight of the man beside whom she had been seated. He had found an equally large woman and a slender, teenaged boy, a slimmer version of himself. The man ruffled the boy's hair as Denise skated by on the side, unobserved. She watched from the corner of her eye as the man and his family gathered his bags and made their way toward the exit doors.

Denise bent her steps in the direction of the shuttle to her connecting flight. A smile came to her lips as she wondered whatever in this strange world could possibly make her feel close to a man like that.

Photo: J. Adrian Wylie

Derek Green

has spent more than a decade as a professional journalist, and a contract consultant for several multinational corporations. His work has taken him to twenty-two countries on six continents. Green was educated at the University of Michigan, where he was a three-time winner of the prestigious Avery and Jule Hopwood Award in creative writing. His fiction and nonfiction have appeared in national magazines and literary journals, and he has taught creative writing and journalism at the university level. The son of an Irish father and Puerto Rican mother, Green is a fluent speaker of Spanish. He lives in Michigan with his wife and son and is currently at work on a novel. *New World Order* is his first book.

Design and Production

Cover and text design by
Kathy Boykowycz

Cover photo: Dubai skyline

Text set in ITC Stone Serif, designed
in 1987 by Sumner Stone

Titles set in Frutiger, designed in
1975 by Adrian Frutiger

Printed by Thomson-Shore of
Dexter, Michigan, on Nature's
Natural, a 50% recycled paper